Chaos Unmasked

Flavie Bauch

Contents

Chapter 1

There are moments in time where everything just falls apart. On the flip side, there are times where everything seems to come together. It was never my intention to have this happen to me, but because the experience happened, there is no way for me to not tell it. The words are like scars that caress my marred body. They weren't there when the story began but was acquired through the hours and hours facing things that before I never even could conjure up in my imagination. I didn't want this to happen but since I had very little choice in the matter, it would only make sense that I make the most of it.

His eyes are menacing yet I know they don't mean to be. He's taunting me with the way he unconsciously carried his self. It's insane to think how I got into this predicament, chained to a chair; feet and arms bound uncomfortably all because I wanted Jamba Juice. Easily, I could make myself intangible but he knows that and put a power concealer pendant around my neck. Those necklaces are usually super cute and are definitely trending on the runway. I think Marc Jacobs made this particular pendant. Did he even make jewelry? It's quite the shame that the necklaces are more of a nuisance than anything else since they smother my powers to embers.

Who is he? That's easy to answer. He's my evil nemesis, secret crush, a person who's more powerful than me, and the guy who wants to kill me; however, most people call him Phantom. Personally, I ship us so hard it hurts, but that's just my opinion that I will never admit because he isn't afraid to flaunt his affection for me. Even though he claims he wants to kill me, Phantom barely breaks my bones. As long as he doesn't exactly know how hard I ship us, we are in the safe zone, and he will never know. I won't even admit that I have the deepest, minuscule, ember of like towards him. If that just so happens to slip out, then my life will be H-E double hockey sticks, and that's saying something because my life really sucks lollipops right now. And N-O I don't exactly know if Phantom actually genuinely likes me or if he wants to play with my heart strings. What I do know is that he's the reason I am currently bound to a really uncomfortable, wooden, and creaky chair. Maybe if I keep shifting my weight and make it squeak long enough he'll snap and let me go?

The idea is worth a shot, so I begin shifting my weight while watching Phantom warily. He hasn't said two words since I woke up, something that is extremely out of character since Phantom is the most popular villain of the world and he knows it, making my life run on his constant chatter and selfishness. (Out of all the superheroes worldwide I and ranked number 186 if you must know.)

Seriously, his arrogance and cocky attitude kills me! Rather than talk or fight, I just watch him pace in front of me. Creak, creak, creak is the only sound in the... abandoned warehouse. How cliché. Why can't he take me to a five-star hotel room that I'm sure he can afford, with an all you can eat buffet? And the chair is literally the only noise in the whole place because Phantom has this uncanny skill of soft footsteps. When he walks, he makes absolutely no sound, which is awesome when he's invisible because not even I can find him. My lead feet, on the other hand, make so much noise I might as well be a giant. And yes, Phantom makes fun of me for it. Did you even have to ask?

The chair creaks and I wonder when he'll get so annoyed and snap. Even if it's a "Stop making that fricken' frackin' noise!" or something, it will make me feel better.

Does Phantom even know I'm awake? I glance at his back, pausing from shifting my weight. He is dressed in his usual black, skinny dress pants, black, shiny dress shoes and a silver button down shirt that must cost a fortune. His black hair is spiked up in the front- his bangs usually so long they fall in his eyes and the sides of his hair are cropped short. Any other boy with that look would look absolutely awful, but somehow Phantom pulls it off easily.

From where I am sitting, his Gluteus Maximus look very nice, which is an added bonus to seeing Phantom- a girl can fantasize all she wants over him. Broad shoulders lean but conditioned body that has a six-pack (Only when he flexes) make up who Phantom is. He's really hot and ultimately glamorous, yet there's this elegant and grace to him that Phantom tries to cover up by unsuccessfully looking like a bad boy. It also doesn't hurt that he treats me like a prince ss... most of the time.

After a moment of silence, Phantom's head whips in my direction, and he stands in from of me, "Finally!" he cries in his sharp voice, and I stare at him like an idiot. We both have sharp voices, making us sound ruder than we try to be.

"Huh?" I respond cleverly, caught off guard, and his cry still resonates through my eardrums.

"You stopped the incessant creaking! Honestly, I was going to kill you if you kept that up any longer," he grumbles.

My mouth twists into a pout, making my shiny lip-gloss worth wearing, "Well then stop pacing! You'll only wear down the wood and create a path, and seriously, an abandoned warehouse? Is that really the best you can do? We've been over this before, and you know I don't like the creepy places you hide our informal meetings," I huff.

"You were drooling and I simply didn't want my silk shirt to get ruined with your drool. This shirt isn't cheap, you know," Phantom scoffs back, pointing to his gray shirt. There is a trace of a smile on his lips.

"I didn't know because clothes are just clothes, and who cares if their name brand or not!" I retort, creaking the chair just so Phantom would cringe, and he doesn't let me down- his face visibly pained for a split second before masking it over with a frown. I smile at that.

"Every time I knock you out, you drool," Phantom points at my black shirt sleeve with a gloved finger. I groan in frustration, there's a puddle of drool on it! Talk about embar-ras-s ing...

"Then here's an easy solution: Don't knock me out," I say snidely as an attempt to keep my nonexistent pride.

"What makes you think I'll stop? Maybe I like knocking you out, and draping your body over my shoulder? Ever thought of that?" he raises an eyebrow, but a curious look passes over his face, lighting his eyes so that they resemble emeralds.

"Well, I don't know! Maybe you care about my math grade because it isn't as high as it should be?" I attempt weakly, false hope lacing my tone. Phantom only shrugs, which isn't a yes or a no. What does a shrug mean in guy language?! I rack my brain for any clue to what that means because it shouldn't mean anything, yet that is how he answers.

"You care about my social life, and kidnapping me means I can't go through with any of my plans with my school mates. Don't you give me that look! I have friends!" I glare at him, since he raised both of his eyebrows, and gave me a quizzical look. Phantom only laughs, and it's a musical sound. I suppose it was a little far fetched that I had a life outside of school and saving the city. I didn't have that many friends, just one girl named Anna Henderson who was the superhero Anigirl. So his assumption was correct. All of his assumptions are usually right.

"You're exceptionally witty today," Phantom muses. I am stunned that he complimented me that I don't have any-thing else to say. "I love that about you. Anyways, I'm such a terrible secret keeper that I just have to tell someone the Brother's newest development," he pauses and waits for me to respond, which I don't even though the suspense is killing me. There's no doubt in my mind that Phantom is, in fact, a superior secret keeper, so the fact that he intends to spill the beans on something huge has me both frozen in terror and elation. The Brothers he was talking about is mostly he and his fellow villain and BFF Rush, but I wonder who else knows this big secret.

I bite my lip to hold in that question. Do I even what to know his little secret, or will it be life altering? If it is life altering then I can see why Phantom is bouncing on the balls of his heels like a little kid.

"Only Rush and I know, as of yet, but we are including you and Anigirl in it... Rush found Anigirl's secret identity," he frowns and studies me. When he sees my lack of reaction because my whole entire brain decided to take a little vacay, disappointment clouds his features. As it sinks in, and the pause draws out, I feel each of my muscles tense up. Anigirl is Anna Henderson, daughter of a very prominent old money family of the east coast. Her family basically adopted me, so I just happen to live with her. And that means that my secret identity could be unwrapped too.

And I absolutely could not let that happen. My civilian life and Phantom could N-E-V-E-R mix. In fact, I am convinced that it would explode if the two lives even thought of mixing together.

"Ah, so you do know her. I can see the recognition in your eyes. Rush felt pretty stupid after figuring it out, you know.

The names Anna and Anigirl are insanely close, not counting the fact she can turn into animals. That's a cruel trick she played on us. I wonder if your name is close to Chaos...?" he trails off, raising an eyebrow. Chaos is my super name, and I don't think it's close to my real name. Rush is like Phantom's best friend, and part of the Brothers, which is a band of evil villains that has been growing rapidly the past year. Most of the time Phantom and Rush work on their own, but occasionally they will join with others to get the job done.

"My name is not even close to Chaos," I growl, glaring at him. I'm too defensive, which he'll take as a lie. It's kind of freaky glaring at him because we have the same piercing green eyes, that are all sharp, and not dull. Actually, Phantom and I share a lot of different traits. When I am not transformed, I have Phantom's jet-black hair. It's only sensible that when Phantom isn't Phantom he has platinum blonde hair- almost white.

He sighs dramatically, "Is that so? How well do you know Anna? Are you two friends? Schoolmates? There is this girl who practically lives at her house... that would be the perfect candidate for you," those eyes, undeterred by my glare, study me closely for the slightest hint that he was right.

I scoff, "As if. Is this really why you kidnapped me? Lame!" Inside I was freaking out. My hands, which were tied together behind my back, clammed up with nerves.

Phantom shrugs his shoulders. If that was all he had to say then he could have waited. "Well, I also wanted to ask you a few questions, things that are off the wall and don't relate to anything in particular. We never really talk, you know. Not once have you and I created a heart to heart conversation, and that is a shame because I know you're cooler than you show," he says nonchalantly.

"And this discussion couldn't wait until summer?" I know it's Friday, but I wanted to do my homework early so Anna and I could save the world all weekend long. Don't get me wrong, being a person of Phantom's interest is a long, lost dream, and I should be honored to carry such a title. I turned my head towards the cargo doors to see the orangey glow of a sunset. So it was getting late already, and I definitely need to be home before my absence is noticed.

"Okay, we can talk even though the power concealer is making me feel like I'm suffocating," I hint at my discomfort, but Phantom rolls his eyes in an uncaring manner. Seriously the threat on my life was beginning to make me freak out even more than I already am. With every passing minute, my breath gets shallower. If this keeps up I'm pretty sure I'll die-not to be over-dramatic or anything. But does Phantom care about it? No. Other than the roll of his eyes, his lips twitch into a smirk. He doesn't think I'll die, but like he's ever worn a power concealer! So it's not like he would know the feeling...

I shift my weight in the chair, making it creak just to see if he'll get upset but he doesn't even flinch. Creak, creak, creak... nada. No reaction whatsoever. I frown up at him, blonde eyebrows furrowing.

"My gosh, you are seriously obnoxious today!" He growls after a moment. I smile full on at him as he turns on his Death Glare in my direction. Oooh, scary! It's about time he cracked, honestly.

Maybe he feels as if he should start a conversation before I do something that he'll really kill me for because Phantom squares his shoulders and becomes suddenly very curious, "Is school hard right now? You know... Do you have a lot of homework are your grades up? Stuff like that," the questions burst out of his mouth.

Cautiously I ask, "Why do you want to know?" Does he really care or does Phantom just want to figure out my secret ID?

His dress shoes lift up a few centimeters off the ground and he is hovering three inches off the ground, but enough clearance not to accidentally touch the floor. I could do that too, but Phantom can hover up to three feet in the air, and I can barely get eleven inches. He's trying to be intimidating by showing me up, but it is a well-known fact that he's more powerful than I am. Truthfully, he goes easy on me when we fight each other because he doesn't want to kill me, as much as he states otherwise.

"Just answer me," he sighs like I'm a five-year-old kid. Oh, I guess I do act like one when I'm Chaos. Phantom just has to deal with that, and I have no sympathy.

"It's the end of the school year, so yeah I'm friggin' busy. The amount of math homework I get each night is substantial, but it's easy to me. My grades are good enough for me not to get in trouble, and this is seriously the longest conversation I've had with anyone since March. You think I'm joking but it's true. And thank you for dealing with my insanity. Needless to say, I appreciate it," I say vaguely. You can never give him too much information in case he'll use it against you. The number one rule is to never trust a villain, no matter the smallest, tiniest, inkling of a crush you may have on said villain.

Phantom hovers so closely to me, leaning in my face. I stiffen, thoughts immediately going to how the nonexistent spectators would view this stance. No matter, I should be concerned with the sense of security and warmth I feel at his close proximity.

I wiggle in the chair, trying to make the rope and zip ties around my wrists more comfortable. It is required that a superhero gets both the itchy rope and the cutting ties since it takes ultimate skill to get out of both before the villain notices. Just moving my wrists make Phantom quickly check the ties to see if I've cut them or something. He knows the only knife I have is in my combat boot that I can't reach. Phantom knows everything he cares to find out.

Before I can think this through I say, "You know it might be easier if you figured out my identity. My life would go down the toilet, but I don't think you will tell the media since you haven't gone to the news channels proclaiming who Anigirl really is."

Phantom stops hovering, feet landing silently on the con-crete. Joy, our legs are lightly brushing each other- that's how close we are. "Why? Why don't you think I am trying to find out who you really are?" he asks.

"You figure out whatever you want to find out. If you know Anna then it's pretty obvious she links to me. I may not be her best of a friend or the girl who lives with her, but I do consider her a good person to be around. The only reason you told me about her is that you don't want to find me. You brought me here to warn me that I should be on guard because you do not want Rush to know and I think you don't want to know because we both know that once you figured out my secret identity, whoever you really are will suddenly waltz into my life and I'm not stupid. I know that you have platinum blonde hair and the same eyes as me, so I'll know who really are. You don't want me to know quite yet. And If you suddenly start hanging around a girl, then what will your Brothers think? They'll connect the dots because they aren't stupid either. All in all, you're trying to protect me and yourself," I nod, happy that I figured out his thought process, It isn't every day I can read Phantom like a book.

And the idea of Phantom trying to protect me makes my heart beat a little faster.

He smiles a small smile, and I know that every word I said was right. But my jaw still hits the floor and I start to giggle crazily, "You're insane! Trying to protect your worse enemy! Phantom is insane, Phantom is insane!" I sing through my fit of laughter.

"You're the insane one, Chaos," his tone is sharper than a blade, and freaking colder than ice could ever be. My giggles die in my throat, and I focus all my attention on him.

"Only Rush and I know about Anigirl- Anna, whatever. There's this villain named Surpass who has created the Brothers you know. However, he has even more villains pledging their support to him every day. And what has become a small cult is now a full on army. That army wants to destroy all the superheroes from off the face of the earth.

Rush and I didn't have to take the new oath because we have apparently proven our loyalty to him. We were in this frenzy to figure out who you two are to protect you. Rush is not the one who really found out Anna's identity, it was me. It was by complete accident, the more I was following your trail, the more it led me to Anna." he gives me a skeptical look.

"There's no possible way you could be Anna. There was no way you could act so mellow at home, and then totally flip around when your Chaos. Besides, between you and me she isn't the brightest person I know. That meant that Anna Henderson was Anigirl because that was the only other option. Tonight you just confirmed an educated guess," Phantom sighs, stuffing his hands in his pockets, and leaning against the wall coolly.

I bite my lips, "Why did Anna come up?" I ask. If what he says is true, and there will be a group of villains setting out to exterminate heroes then we are all in deep trouble. And who else could follow the same trail as Phantom that misguides them to Anna? That would put her in the ultimate danger. Villains haven't banded together since the prohibition fiasco, it was unheard of, but I couldn't deal with that yet. I shove aside those thoughts. Protect Anna first. Potential death can be procrastinated until a later time.

Phantom wrings his hands nervously, trying to come up with the right words to answer my question. "Honestly? I have no idea how or why she of all people came up. When you aren't Chaos you have black hair, correct? Well, Anna has brown hair and that kind of helped. I even snuck into the high school's information to try and find you. I'll bet money that you're a girl who has a small record, black hair, and green eyes, with horrendous grades- although you said that your grades were fine. The thought that you might not have a record, and you keep up your grades never occurred to me, and of course that would be true," He pauses, letting me indulge on all the information. He likes to talk, and feed me information, but sometimes it could be too much to handle. I nod that he was right.

"I have a record and decent grades," I assert. A little mishap with a gang leader freshman year resulted in a seven-day suspension, and B's and C's were all I could handle at this point in my life.

"I'll keep that in mind," Phantom cracks a rare small smile- even showing off his perfectly straight and white teeth. "As soon as I figured out who Anigirl really is, I didn't tell Rush because I didn't want him to go right to Anna and tell her. If Anigirl knew she would have gone straight to tell you and Rush would overhear that conversation and bam- you're in immense danger. But then he knew I knew something and proposed the idea that if we wait a few days and laid low for a little while you two would eventually go patrol the city. When you take a break we'd snatch you up, and tell you both miles apart from each other. So I told Rush what I knew, and we laid low, which was fine since our lives got freaking busy this past week anyway."

"So you took us from Jamba Juice to tell us this? Not nice," I grumble, but inside I am glad that Anna isn't here with me.

"Right. Why Jamba Juice? There's that pastry shop down-town that's super delish. Try the crème Brule, okay?" Phantom rants.

"Does it matter?" I scoff.

He ignores me. I sigh, "Well it's been a good conversation, but I really got to run. Can this count as a date? I'm totally counting it as a date. You can untie me, it's Friday, but math homework beckons," I visibly flinch, worried that I might have given key information away. Is it normal to do homework on Friday? It's not like I have any friends to hang out with... besides Anna.

Phantom smirks and a wave of annoyance washes over me. Did he not know that I am wasting my time here? Anna had to forcibly drag me out of the house to patrol in the first place.

But instead of untying me, Phantom only leans in close. So close that it's impossible not to inhale the sweet mint of his breath. Our eyes unnervingly lock, and I am frozen. Phantom tilts his head to the side, and I have an internal war with myself. Chaos doesn't want to be kissed, but Kelsey definitely wants Phantom to put his lips to hers ASAP. He was the king of sexy, and if he wants to kiss me, I shouldn't complain, besides, it's his choice if he wants to break the villain code.

Phantom's finger slide along my jaw and I wish we both didn't have to wear gloves so I could feel his silky skin, I've felt his skin before. It was a long time ago and an evil villain called Nickol shot my shoulder. Phantom took me to his hideout (that he doesn't share with Rush) and pulled it out.

A shiver passes through my body as I wait patiently for his torture to stop.

"Chaos, you're so powerful, yet you don't let me teach you how to hone your powers. Why I wonder," he does one of his infamous long pauses. Maybe I should answer but I am in no condition to do anything right now. My heart pounds loudly against my ribs.

Phantom smiles and closes the distance between our lips. His hand cradles the back of my head, mussing my hair. The ropes and zip ties dig painfully into my wrists but my mind is only focused on him. I never want Phantom to pull away and he doesn't.

I'm the one who breaks it off. The spell crumbles and Phantom steps away with a pleased and amused look on his face.

"What was bad about that?" He mutters mostly to himself. Nothing was wrong, in fact, quite the opposite was true. It felt incredible to kiss him.

He fingers the pendant that conceals my powers. My heart thuds panicked in my chest, but he skillfully picks the pendant up so his fingers don't brush me. Carefully Phantom lifts the chain over my head and takes it off. A surge of power envelops me and I sigh in content. There's something oddly comforting in having my powers back.

Almost immediately I turn intangible, my molecules vibrating roughly, and I stand up, ropes and zip ties falling to the floor. As I stand I covertly fix the major wedgie that was created a long time ago with all the shifting around. Phantom states it's time to go for both of us.

"It's been a real slice, but Pre Cal- uh math, can't do its self... unfortunately," I snicker to try to cover up the slip. If he knew I was in Pre Calc then my cover was thinner than before. "See you when you try destroying Fields again, Phantom!" I salute him.

Kelsey Jerrs is the smart one, Chaos is... pure chaos.

"You cannot afford to slip up, Chaos. If you do, it'll make it easier for me to figure you out. Have fun with Pre Calc. Should I be offended that you find math more exciting than me?" he laughs at himself, "That's not even possible."

I growl and slip through the warehouse wall to freedom. Where was I? Phantom follows me and points into the direction of the Jamba Juice.

"Don't forget to try the crème Brule!" He calls after me as I run from him.

Chapter 2

It was late into the night when I finally saw the mansion. It wasn't my home but my friend's. I live with her because of my special familial circumstances. Anna's family took me in when I was ten years-old, the time Mrs. Henderson met my Mother for the first time. At the moment I basically already lived with the Hendersons so it wasn't a big deal to me. When I was twelve, Mom got sent to the mental institution where she is now. Nobody believes me when I tell them she is possessed. It was the hardest decision for me to make, sending her to that specific hospital. I considered letting Chaos ruin the whole thing by taking Mom away, but that would not be a heroic thing to accomplish so I didn't. She's still my family even if she tries to kill me.

I work on Pre Calc like a madwoman. Math has always been easy for me as it just makes complete sense. For Anna though, math was another language, and I end up helping her with basic algebra. The only time I had a struggle with math was in Freshman Honors Geometry, but I still got a mid-A for my final grade.

Around eleven-thirty I am putting my textbook away when I hear the door to the bathroom open, signaling that Anna is home. She must have turned into an ant to get through the front door, or left her bedroom window slightly ajar. Both of our rooms are in the basement of this oversized mansion, but there are windows and fire escapes that we use on a daily basis to sneak out of the house when we need to hero up and if a person were to walk down the spiral staircase that reaches all three levels of the house then they would see the biggest entertainment room. Free Pac-Man, two mini flat screens for assorted video-game consoles that only Anna touches, a huge flat screen for TV and movies, leather couch and matching chairs, a decked out soda bar, and a mini fridge with all-you-can-eat Ben & Jerry's ice cream, and a bookshelf with a few books, tons of games, and a sufficient supply of movies that Anna and I have collected over the years.

The basement is basically our lair. An unspoken rule in the house is that Anna and I cannot go to the master suite (which takes over half of the third floor), unless we are cleaning it, and Anna's parents rarely come down stairs. The main level is all fair game.

I get up from the couch to head to my room. Anna is in the bathroom with the door closed so I do not see her. Shutting the door behind me, I dress for bed in my pink $E=MC2$ pajamas. I do not consider pink as a color I would wear on a daily basis, but I must admit, these pajamas are super nerdy. When I hear the bathroom's faucet turn on I hurry, pulling on a huge tee that states "Oh crap she's up! -Devil" on it, and turn off the lights so I can act like I've been asleep for hours. Anna won't buy it once she realized I haven't brushed my teeth (I can't sleep unless my mouth is minty fresh, okay?) but if Phantom or Rush is watching her they won't know that.

I muse my black hair before I slowly creak open the door. For effect, I blink as the bathroom door is open and light 'pierces' my eyeballs. "You're home," I yawn at Anna as she steps to the side of the sink for me.

She wets her toothbrush with one hand, the other hand pushing her corn silk hair behind her ear, "Yup. I got so caught up with Ryan and Luis that I didn't notice the time," she yawns and sticks the toothbrush in her mouth. Ryan and Luis are real friends of Anna's but they never hang out after school, so the names are also coded for Phantom and Rush. Ryan is code for Rush, and Luis is code for Phantom.

"You must have had lots of fun. I didn't even hear you come down the stairs," I say, nudging her shoulder lightly.

Those brown eyes slice into mine, "Well I did," she shrugs. What do shrugs even mean? I huff heavily. Shrugs are not answers. They are neither yes nor no. Why do people answer with a shrug? I don't even think people realize what they are doing whenever they shrug. I know Anna didn't realize that she even did the motion. Instead of railing about it though, I let her brush her teeth in peace and as she rinses I start brushing.

"Kelsey?" she asks softly before leaving me alone.

"Wfth?" I ask totally expecting her to get what I meant to say with a toothbrush and foam in my mouth. When she doesn't answer right away, my sharp green eyes meet hers.

She must have decided not to tell me, since she takes a sharp breath, "Don't tell me you were working on homework on a Friday night again!"

What? Talk about a random topic of conversation. I always do my homework Friday night because if I don't then I never will. Anna, on the other hand, waits until Sunday night to even open her backpack. Instead of looking like she totally threw me for a loop, I give her the best look of innocence I can muster- which isn't a lot, and I realize that I must resemble a chipmunk so I don't keep the act for long. Looking like Phantom means that you also look like a Punk rocker who's searching for their next fix- especially when I get no sleep and I have bags under my eyes. It's anything but innocent. Even if my pajamas were nerdy, my jet black hair and piercing green eyes were too hard and sharp. Seriously, how can Phantom not know that I, Kelsey Jerrs, am Chaos? He has to be blind in order for his brain not to figure it out. Anxiety sinks into the pit of my stomach like the Titanic sunk into the ocean. Is Phantom here? Is Rush watching Anna interact with me at this very moment?

Before I have time to go into a full out panic attack, Anna lightly puts a hand on my shoulder. "Kells it'll be okay, you know," she says as an attempt to soothe me. Huh, I must have let my panic show on my face.

I rinse my mouth, realizing that having a toothbrush dangle out of my mouth and not brushing it is very unbecoming. My mouth is minty fresh anyways. Anna leaves to do whatever her heart desires, which I know is not sleeping.

I put my toothbrush away and turn to leave. As I do I catch a glimpse of myself in the mirror. My hair is absolutely ridiculous so I run a brush through it before deciding to braid the shoulder length hair. When I look into the mirror I see Phantom, and when Anna looks into a mirror she sees a pixified, petite Rush.

Rush... That villain can turn into every animal like Anna, but Rush has figured out a way to be wooden, or organic things too. Thank goodness there hasn't been anyone who can turn into everything at once! Scientists deem it impossible, but super powers are impossible to have. Truthfully, I think someone out in the world can be any object, but the public would be out of their minds with terror so they keep it under wraps. My power isn't rejoiced over either, (hence my rank as #183) and I just walk through walls, turn invisible, and shoot green energy out of my palms!

How the flip is Phantom ranked #1? Well, along with his amazing charm (That apparently I lack even though I look just like him), Phantom also has money, style, grace, elegance, and plays with all the ladies. I do not like the paparazzi, don't have much elegance and poise, am studying too hard to have time to be a player, and I don't have money.

Wow, I am seriously lacking.

To top it all off, Phantom likes to work with the broad shouldered, football player bodied, rude and ultimately stupider than a bag of rocks: Rush.

Anigirl ranks higher than Rush! At #5 is where Anna ranks in the charts, and #12 is Rush. Anna says 'Oh it's not big deal Kells,' or 'It's just a number, it doesn't determine your happiness,' but I know that the press just hates me because I am not romantically inclined to such a Greek God. Anigirl isn't afraid to kiss Rush though, and the press eats it up.

I enter my room. My room is most commonly referred to as the Black Hole since I went through a Goth stage for a few years. Anna has attempted to make it brighter by getting a purple bedspread, but I personally think I need yellow in here. There's a walk in closet that mostly has everything but clothes in it, a dresser that holds all of me and Chaos's clothes, and a black leather couch that holds so many blankets and books.

I lay on my bed, pushing all of my textbooks and scattered papers off the bed and onto the floor. It creates a huge pile of mess on the ground, but I couldn't care. In my life, there were bigger fish to fry. I hear Anna go up the stairs, which was close to my room.

"You're so powerful, yet you won't let me teach you. Why?" Phantom's question rings through my head.

Why? I haven't the slightest idea how to answer that. Maybe it was the way my heart sputtered uncontrollably whenever I was around him. If I couldn't bear fighting him, if our skin ever made contact, then all my... Romantic feelings would be as clear as crystal to him. And if Phantom ever knew about my feelings then he would reciprocate, and my life would be thrown into the darkest abyss if turmoil one could scarcely understand.

So letting Phantom teach me how to fight is a no-no.

And that wasn't including hiding my secret identity!

My life is so complicated. Seriously, never become a super-hero if you want a normal, boring life.

I snuggle under the covers and hope that maybe tomorrow would be much better. At least Anna would have a good day, go shopping or something fun. I would catch up on my T.V. shows, try out the bakery that Phantom said to and hopefully get some study time with Anna because Heaven knows she needs it.

If Phantom really cared about protecting us, then he wouldn't appear in my life tomorrow.

Ha! One could only hope for a miracle, and that would be number one on my miracle list. I mean, we didn't fight each other every day. I am pretty sure Phantom is a student somewhere, whether that is high school or college.

Sometimes he would say, "Ah Chaos! Can we get a rain check for the rest of the week? I have a huge exam I need to study for and if we studied together I would imagine that we wouldn't get any studying done at all."

And then I would reply "Yes! Thank goodness yes! Take as long as you want off."

But that Friday night he would appear, my break would be over and he would be as clingy as ever before because he 'missed me.'

Talk about a load of crap.

Saturday morning rolls around. I open my heavy eyelids and look at the clock. Ugh, it's 6:30 in the morning. Can't I ever sleep in?

No, it's impossible for me to sleep in. I've always had that problem, ever since I was a little kid. Even though my body desperately needs the rest, I can never sleep past the sunrise.

My body is sore, even though I don't know what I did last night that required my muscles. It sucks being a superhero. Everyone expects so much from you, but they don't realize that you're also just like them. Just because one has extra power doesn't make them inhuman or Superman. It's a common mistake the population makes all the dang time. Do more, be faster, be prettier, be different all the time because you're a super and nothing you can do in your life will ever change that no matter how hard you try because your DNA is twisted with radioactive chemicals that doctors cannot determine a name for.

Actually, there aren't any radioactive chemicals in my DNA but in some people's there is. I believe Anna's has a malfunction of some type.

But right now I am everything but super, in my nerd pajamas and midnight hair that is currently sticking out in all different directions. Maybe today I'll visit that place Phantom said to try. It was worth a shot, and if he brought it up, it had to be good food.

I sigh and then get up to go upstairs as quietly as possible without being intangible. That wouldn't be fun if the security cameras the Henderson's may or may not have put up caught my secret on tape. Anna is a freaky light sleeper, whereas I slept through the fire alarms one time in my apartment before my parents were locked up in jail. And unfortunately, Anna's room is directly under the stairs. The slanted ceiling had posters of us as superheroes, and of course the boys too. She did have an obsession with Phantom and Rush too, you know.

Mrs. Henderson is already at the counter, eating a 'super healthy and delicious' spinach smoothie. She's the queen of healthy stuff. Every morning at seven Mrs. Henderson takes a five-mile 'jog' and then works out until noon. She is insane, and her diet reflects her insanity.

I snagged my Cocoa Puffs the chef gets just for me. Lumar, the chef, loves me a lot since I hung out with him while in a culinary class at school.

Anna's mom looks at me, a smile on her red lips, "Everyday you eat that pure sugar. Why don't you try this smoothie?" she urges.

My eyes roll, "Ugh, I hate veggies."

"That's not true," she frowns at me.

I shrug. Maybe it is and maybe it isn't. I definitely hate spinach that wasn't drowning in ranch.

"So, Anna and you have any plans for today?" she asks. Mrs. Henderson has been my personal guardian angel for years. She's like the only person in this world that I tell everything (except the Chaos part) to. For a few years, I treated her like crap, since she made me quit smoking cold turkey. It was the hardest thing I've ever done, but she helped me through it. Unfortunately, that meant that I was under house arrest until my cravings were dull enough that I wouldn't shake even if I walked past another person who was smoking.

"Well, there's this pastry shop downtown that I want to try. Do want something? I'm thinking about brings some snacks back," I answer honestly, pouring milk into my bowl and stirring my cereal around before taking a bite.

She would want a lemon tart, I think.

"Well, if there's anything lemon, then I guess I'll cheat," she gives in. I smirk, pleased with myself. Not even Anna or her dad could get Mrs. Henderson to cheat off her 'diet' thingy.

"Well, when you're going to go out, just text me. I won't respond, but at least I'll know where you are," she says. That's an unspoken rule in this house. If you go out, you gotta at least text someone where you are. It sucks when I'm trying to lace up my Chaos boots and texting with my phone hallways in my mouth that Anna and I are going to a 'football game' or something. Anna usually lets me text her mom, so our stories match up and she doesn't have to deal with lying to her mom. I lie all the time, so it's not a big deal to me.

"I think you should cheat more. You weigh less than I do," I told Mrs. Henderson, poking her ribs as she walked past me.

"That's because you eat that kind of sugar crap," she countered in a teasing manner.

I laugh. It's also because I need some padding so when my body makes contact with the road, or whatever my body encounters at 30 miles an hour speeds, I wouldn't die or be totally broken.

Besides, Phantom said that he didn't like girls who were completely skinny. He said that "Girls are more alluring when they have at least some meat on their bones. Plus, if I were to take a girl to a really fancy restaurant and she orders a freaking salad then I know she's not for me."

He also expanded on that idea, but I'll censor those irreverent thoughts.

But Mrs. Henderson doesn't know any of that, so in this case, I smile sweetly and bat my eyelashes.

She lightly flicks my cheek, "You're real cute, Kells."

"I know," I tease, shoveling another spoonful into my mouth. She sighs, then puts her cup in the sink and gets out of the kitchen to leave for her jog. I quickly finish up my breakfast, thankful that Anna is not up yet, and then go through one of the many hallways that branch from the front entrance of the mansion, and then meet the spiral staircase and go down it.

I enter my room and dress in a black maxi skirt and a U2 band shirt. It's comfortable, yet one of the best outfits I own. I go to the vanity in the bathroom, where I apply a small amount of black eyeliner and mascara and then as quietly as possible brush my teeth. Anna will ignore the sound of me brushing but not for a long time.

Quickly I finish up and then run back upstairs and out of the house before Anna even had the chance to come out of her room. It's not that I'm going out to somewhere I don't want her to come with, but something in my head just didn't want her to tag along. Besides, I rationalize; I'll bring home a cupcake or whatever she wants.

By the front door is a small hall closet that is hardly ever opened. In it were two small backpacks: one that held a change of Chaos's clothes, and the other a change of Anigirl's. I take my black and gray backpack and put it on. It's super cute with everything I wear, and I put my wallet in the front pocket a little while ago. Everyone thinks it's like a purse, but they couldn't be more wrong.

I step out of the house and decide to take a cab. It would be less stress if I didn't drive into town and if something superhero happened, then I would still be able to take a cab and not have to drive the (easily traceable) car home. Call me crazy, fine. Anna states more than a hundred times that I am paranoid. But if Phantom hasn't figured out my identity, then my irrational fears serve me well. Anna doesn't know that she can't say that anymore.

"Where to, miss?" the driver asks.

I tell him the name of the bakery and then wait patiently as he pulls into the busy road. Taxis are always in this area since the people living in the mansions tip extremely well so I wasn't surprised to get one of my own so quickly.

When the car pulls up to the bakery I smile and pay the driver. Money was never an issue since I get a weekly allowance of twenty bucks a week and I never buy anything. My debit card alone has way more money than I would ever use in my lifetime thanks to the Henderson's generosity that I tried hard to repay.

I step out of the cab and inhale the scents of honey, warm bread, and sugar. It's so sickly sweet, and my stomach roars with hunger. I clutch my stomach. Did Phantom say to try the crème Brule? As I enter, there's a podium with a girl my age behind it. I think she goes to my school, and she might be in one of my classes, but I never pay attention to other people in classes so I can't be sure.

"Hello, and welcome to Crumble! Just one?" the girl asks.

"Uh yeah. Sure. Whatever," I say, tugging at my black hair nervously. Why was it so formal if it was just a bakery?

She leads me to a seat reserved for two, and I almost wish that Anna was with me so I wouldn't be alone. What if Phantom was here?

She hands me a one-sided menu, and I can't help but feel strange in a U2 concert T-shirt when everyone was extremely well dressed. It's just a cafe!

I peruse it, and sure enough, they have a berry, cinnamon, and original crème Brule. What's the difference? I didn't seem to know. And yes, they have a lemon tart that was much bigger than I expected. Sweet. Their assortment of cupcakes was overwhelming, so I got Anna a strawberry one.

When the waiter came up, I wasn't anticipating him. A middle aged man with thinning hair took my order, and in less than five minutes came back with my food.

"Holy cow," I mutter, rolling the to-go bag up since the waiter didn't do it. My creme brulee is at the side of the bag, a mini spoon already dipped in it. I take my first bite and a blueberry pops in my mouth. It's so delicious. I melt as I shovel in another bite. Needless to say, I will never be satisfied with another one's attempt of this dessert, since I am in complete bliss.

Fancy or not, this is the place to go. Crumble.

After a few minutes I am basically licking the little plastic cup clean... Until there is a loud screech of a megaphone and then I hear "COME OUT, COME OUT AND PLAAAAY!" in a guttural voice that belonged to only one person in this whole world. The half man, half gorilla, failed experiment called Rilla Man.

I say an unrepeatable word under my breath, and get up from my seat. I guess you go to that podium to pay since a few other couples have done so. Quickly I pay, but the girl grips my arm.

"Don't go out there!" she warns.

I just shake her off, "I have to get home by eleven," I lie as an excuse to leave.

"It's dangerous out there!" she cries as I open the door to leave.

Only if you can't turn intangible, I think with a small smirk.

You see, even with Rilla Man's inhuman strength and monkey calls, I am too awesome for him. Super strength is no good unless it hits a target, and I usually never get hit.

When you're a superhero, you get used to the fact that you have to change in the strangest of places. Usually, I prefer to dumpster dive into a recycling bin, but Anna and I both have been in strange circumstances where we had to change in an uninhabited homeless person's home, or in the bathroom of a gas station that was seriously nasty. We have loads of nightmare stories.

But, luckily for me, the little shop next to Crumble was a Home and Cards shop. That means, no matter how small the trash bin was, it was rarely used. So I hopped into the recycling bins, trying as little as humanly possible not to breathe. Just because it was a recycling bin doesn't mean it smelled like flowers, and I banged my head on the metal lid three times while attempting to change clothes before I emerged as Chaos. There was a familiar tingle as my body started to change a little bit, too. My hair was now platinum blonde and I wrapped a studded belt around my hips and laced up my boots. The carry out bag was stuffed with my other clothes in my small backpack, and I hoped with all my might that Rilla Man wouldn't crush them.

I strut confidently out into the street, shaking my long hair. That gorilla wouldn't know what had hit him, plus, there wasn't Anigirl, so he'd be distracted while he searched for her. Just because he was half man didn't mean he had a smart brain.

"Ahhh, Chaos! I have smelled you since you first arrived here!" His voice booms.

Oh yeah, he has 'ape' sense of smell. He probably sensed me as Kelsey! I frown at the thought.

"Hello to you, too!" I plaster on an ultra fake smile and whip my platinum hair to the side.

He growls and then charges right towards me. My eyes widen, and then I turn intangible as he plows through me.

I laugh, and turn around to face him again, "Seriously, Ape man, I could do this all morning!"

"I could think of a few... other things... that you and I could do alllll morning, Chaos," an ice-cold voice states humorously. I shiver from the blast of that icy attack. Phantom. It is impossible for me not to feel his eyes scan from my toes to the top of my hair at the most excruciatingly slow pace.

Rilla Man takes another charge towards me since he thinks I'm preoccupied with Phantom and goes through me once again.

I don't care about him though because my main focus is on Phantom as he confidently struts across the street towards me. I note that he is also wearing a studded belt with his dressy slacks and immediately regret my choice of belt. But I guess he didn't notice because the first thing he says is, "I see you took my advice? Pity I missed you come in to taste the delectable creme brulee. You see I thought I set my alarm clock for seven-thirty, but alas I did not. Sad day for me." He frowns and stops walking a good foot away from me. Rilla man keeps running through the both of us, his gorilla face scrunched with fury.

"Sucks to be you," I simply state. It's not like I care if he saw me or not.

"Was it good? Did you get something for Anigirl as well? Their iced sugar cookies are to die for as well," Phantom inquires with his hands in the pockets of his black dress pants.

"It's none of your business," I retort.

There are screams as Rilla Man starts to literally tear up the street. I wince then run full speed towards that stupid ape. A small green orb glows in my hand, and I throw it at the villain. It strikes him on the head, and I use that small window of opportunity as Rilla Man shakes off the pain to kick him on the ground. That kick used seriously all of my weight to get the thing to fall. He's stunned so I punch him in the face as the police appear, their sirens wailing in my ears.

"Ugh guh-ross!" I cry, shaking my hand with my 'gross face' plastered on. There was a glob of gorilla boogies all over my knuckles.

Phantom laughs, "You punched a gorilla in the nose, and look at what happened! Absolutely priceless face, BTW."

I am so mad that I just glare at him as Phantom takes out his iPhone and snaps a picture. Of course, I am still straddling Rilla Man and so I get off of him. At least he was unconscious, unlike someone to my right who I would like very much to hit in the nose.

"On your knees! Both of you!" the cops cry with their guns pointed at me and Phantom. My eyes widen, and on instinct, I raise my hands up.

A gun gets fired, and Phantom lunges at me and we sink through the street underground. My body hums differently than normal because he is forcing me to be intangible. I fight against him, but Phantom has a crazy grip on the back of my shirt, also clutching the back of my bra and I worry that it'll come undone.

"Where's my backpack?" I realize, my body freezing.

Phantom pauses, and I also note that he stopped walking, or falling deeper underground.

I turn intangible and shake him off, heading back up. Being underground is kind of scary. It's pitch black, and there's the fear that if you turn normal then you'd immediately die is no fun either.

But of course, he's faster than I am. As I disappear and head to the surface he's already up. But he didn't turn invisible and the cops have their guns out. As silently as I can,

I run to where Rilla Man used to lie but now he is moved onto a tow truck. My backpack! Rilla Man must have smashed it! When I touch the straps it turns invisible also, and then I rummage for the take out bag. To my dismay, the tart was semi crumbled, and the strawberry frosting is all over the little cupcake container.

"Nooooo!" I wail, turning visible. Everyone looks at me. I look at them back. "Can't a girl get a break? Now I'm pissed off. I'm going home, have a good day, officers!" I turn and stomp though that Home and Cards shop into the back alley again, and change in the same recycling can again, back into my U2 shirt and maxi skirt again.

Then I fix my skirt and the major wedgie I got from climbing out of the recycling bin and catch a cab back home.

Stupid cupcakes. Stupid Phantom. Stupid superhero life. I chant to myself after dragging my sorry rear end out of bed on a Tuesday when, the night before, Phantom decided to wreck havoc all up in my life.

Chapter 3

Last night I was doing Pre Calc homework, working with notation crap, outside Mr. and Mrs. Hederson's room in their little 'waiting area' with a front room set of plushy couches, and a coffee table. Nobody was home except for me and Anna- my partner in crime (sometimes literally) who was in our 'secret lair' of the house's basement supposedly working on her vocabulary flash cards. Right after school, we worked on her math, so at least that was already finished. But while I was dozing in between intricate math problems in the silence when I heard Anna shriek so loudly, even I could hear it.

I started, standing up so fast, that the text book and papers fell on my feet, making me cry out in pain. That textbook was heavy!

I limped down the spiral staircase down to the basement, where Anna was running and Superman-ed face first on the couch.

Raising an eyebrow I asked, "Anna, I know this is a basement, but the couch is not first base so what happened?"

She laughed, "Stop being so weird, saying stuff like that. Does the basement look like a baseball diamond?"

That retort made me smile widely, "I don't know, you're the one sliding around."

"Suck it!" she hissed. I knew that she wouldn't answer my question about what happened, because of her sour attitude. Anna never has a sour attitude unless it was the last week of the month when her period started and she had major cramps.

"O...kay? Who peed in your Cheerios?" I stuck out my tongue at her and slowly backed away.

"KELSEY IMMA KIIIIILLL YOU!" she literally roared at me.

I placed a hand over my heart and took a deep breath like I had gotten impaled, "Ohmawerd! Someone save me from Anna's animalistic wrath! I swear I didn't tinkle in her Cheerios! Anna doesn't even like Cheerios!" I cried while grasping the staircase and running up it.

I stopped when I realized that she wasn't following me.

Only later did Anna tell me that Phantom was in the basement, and he popped out of nowhere which was why she screamed. Apparently, he was just 'checking up on pretty ladies' which was a lie. He probably couldn't handle being invisible for any longer, which only happened to Phantom once every... oh, every five years or so. But to me, it happened all the flippin' time.

Now I was sleeping in my English class when we were supposed to read a chapter of the class's book that I had previously read. The academy, with an obscure name of someone who had a seriously strange spelling to their last name, required a uniform with a long black skirt that wasn't pleated- thank goodness, and a white button down shirt with a gray vest or coat. Vests make my armpits hurt, so I gave all of mine to Anna, who says that sweater vests make her look smarter in a non-nerd related way... whatever that meant.

"Nice of you to join room 410, Miss Jerrs," the teacher looked over her half moon glasses at me.

"Ah, sorry," I apologized, hurrying to open the book as fast as possible and pretending to read it.

"King Macbeth is insane!" a girl stage whispered next to me, looking at the other girl on the other side of me. Great, every day these two girls talk while I am stuck between them. Talk about boring.

"I know! He kind of reminds me of one of your boyfriends. Remember John?" Girl 2 asked.

Girl 1 gasped, "Oh my, yeah! Yeah, he's totally Macbeth crazy!"

Honey, you do not understand the play if you think King Macbeth is like your boyfriend, I want to jump in, but I didn't.

"And his wife is like Marley Fern!" Girl 1 added. Who on earth was Marley Fern? Was she manipulative and greedy?

"Ew. I totally hate that Fern girl," Girl 2 makes a face.

And I was in the middle of them. Always excluded, yet always in the middle of things that I don't want to deal with.

Fern... Did I know a girl with the last name of Fern? The name sounds a bit familiar.

Personally, I thought that the king and his wife were a lot like my parents. Killing people for their gain and stuff like that. It was one of the reasons I took the book home to read it through, even if I did not read a single book all my high school life before, let alone Shakespeare.

A girl could only hope that the dead people haunted her parents while they were in the maximum security prison.

Is that a strange thought? If Anna heard me say something like that she'd give me a serious tongue lashing saying things like, "Kelsey! They are your parents, and you love them! Don't think otherwise! I don't care if they've murdered hundreds of teenagers nationwide to get drugs! They're getting over their addictions anyways!"

And that is the last thing I needed in my life.

"Emerald Cardinale looked at me today!" girl 1 whispers a little bit quieter.

Ah, they always bring up that boy. He doesn't attend this academy- I don't even think he goes to school. How old was he? Anyways, Emerald and Girl 1 lived by each other, although that could mean that he lived five blocks away from her, I don't care how close he really lived because that would be useless information.

"No way! That's the third time this week!"

"Yeah, I swear he likes me!"

"Girl, I have to sleep over on Friday so I could see him too!" Girl 2 squealed.

"Miss Backett, Jerrs, and Hardy. Must I tell you three to be quiet and read again or will you just do whatever you're supposed to do for once in your lives?" the teacher asks. I really despised her funky half moon glasses. Why did she wear glasses if she was looking over them all the dang time?

And of course, my last name was grouped with the two who really were talking even though I didn't say a peep. How frustrating.

I huff under my breath and bury my nose in the play. I usually always slept on reading days, since I finish the book in three days. What was the interesting part was when Miss Benson would dive so deeply and intimately into the plot or the reasons the characters acted the way they did, why Macbeth had to kill his friend. That was the reason why I was here.

Girl 1 and 2 went back to reading, smiles on their faces as they thought about Emerald rather than the play.

Emerald Cardinale's family was extremely rich. I knew that Miss Benson was secretly dating the oldest brother named Hayden. There were five boys, age thirty-one to twelve- Hayden, Jonah, Noah, Mark, and then little Brigg. They were the third richest family in the world and had a mansion that was even bigger than the Henderson's. I've gone to their lavish Christmas parties they threw each year, and that's how I knew that Miss Benson was hitting on Hayden.

They made a super cute couple. Miss Benson was in her mid-twenties so Hayden wasn't too old for her. Whenever the couple had a date, the whole school could tell and my class usually weaseled the facts from her with as much detail as possible.

When the bell to leave class finally rings, I hadn't even turned the page of the book that I've been staring at blankly.

I gather my belongings, holding the book in my arms like the nerds did because my backpack is already zipped shut so what was the point of putting the book in it when the next class-Pre Calc- is just in the other building?

A smile creeps on my face when I realize that it was my absolute favorite class of the day. Math is easy, math is fun, math is my entire world. What can a person do with math? Everything.

Practically skipping to my next class, I catch myself thinking about what Phantom had said that one night in the warehouse. How I can't afford to slip up as Chaos or as Kelsey. I had slipped up big time last night, not noticing that Phantom was in the room. Usually, I could feel his energy but last night I didn't. That scared me big time. Was I being sloppy? Anna's well-being cannot afford my sloppiness.

I slip behind my desk and put my elbows on the table, fingers grasping my black hair. Mr. Monroe wasn't in the classroom and there wouldn't be the class until a few seconds after the tardy bell.

Everything is so hard. The danger that loomed beyond the horizon scared me since Phantom made me aware of it. Could Anna tell that something big was being planned? And then there was the fact that everyday villains like Gorilla man that I wasn't sure was part of Phantom's circle or not. Those villains never committed serious crimes, never had enough power to even try half the things Phantom did every night.

I needed to talk to him tonight no matter what. I needed to evade Anna and somehow find that elusive man. How am I supposed to find someone who is literally a phantom when they don't want to be found? I mean, he's the one that shows up whenever he wants to torment me.

Plus, I had to endure the school life before I could do any sleuthing or find any clues to my questions. Of course, Phantom wouldn't give me a straight answer, but at least it was something rather than nothing.

Mr. Monroe stands at the front of the room and began to speak. I attempted to listen as he handed out the new monthly homework calendars. Those calendars were the only reason I wasn't failing the class. By doing as much Pre Calc as I could on the nights that I had time to do homework meant that I taught myself all the precepts that Mr. Monroe was babbling about.

And Anna's mom wonders why I didn't take a college course. There isn't any time for me to fit in High School and College. Rarely, very rarely, did I have time to relax and take a nap after I finished my homework and house chores. (Mrs. Henderson doesn't let the maid clean downstairs so we can 'learn' to clean up after ourselves.)

We get our homework with fifteen minutes left in class. Mr. Monroe likes to give us at least some time at the end of class to start on it, so we can ask questions or discuss what we don't really understand. I work furiously until the bell rang.

Then finally, I was free to go. I almost cry as I scurry off campus, sending a quick text to Anna telling her not to wait for me. Phantom knows everything, and I needed his answers right away. He has to be home since the public and the private school was out of session now- if he even is a high school student, which I'm not sure.

Practically running down the sidewalk to get to the corn fields at the back of the school, I slow down. There is no need to look suspicious.

It's chilly, so rather than change with a few stalks of corn to cover me, I just slip on a black hoodie and call it good with black ankle boots which were all in my backpack. (I know, those items take up a lot of space!)

I let out a long sigh, hoping that I can find Phantom. If he isn't out tonight then I didn't know what I would do. Maybe I'll save a few robberies or stop car crashes on the main street like I used to do before Phantom sauntered into my freaking life.

Before Anna was in deep dog crap.

I run my fingers through my long white hair. It's pretty silky because of Anna's shampoo expertise. She gets this exotic blend of many spices and fruit that supposedly are really good for hair. Whatever.

Being Chaos is always amusing to me. Sometimes, people won't notice who I am until I use my superpowers or sometimes people freak out and go all fangirl over me, begging me to touch them or sign their arm or something odd. Anna loves her fans, she has perfected her Anigirl signature to look like a paw print, and not even close to her real handwriting. Phantom is amazing with his fans, although he'd rather die than let those people touch him. He just goes through them when they get in his way. Rush likes to joke around with his fans. Me? Well, I just smile and wave, avoiding contact and not answering reporter's questions. I believe that there's a meme of me that's all "this is what silence looks like" with my face. Oh well, what can a girl do?

The itchy corn brushes on my sweatshirt, making it messy with the dust and dirt that are on the leaves. I try patting my shirt clean, but it only makes it worse. Phantom loves the corn fields so I'm hoping that he will take a mid afternoon stroll.

Letting my feet levitate off the floor, I rise above the field, hoping to get attention from a certain someone.

I put up my guard, waiting for Phantom's sharp voice to say something like "Don't you look like poo today," or something. But of course, there isn't any sign of him. How annoying. But standing in the silence with nothing to better me except the corn stalks brushing against my sweatshirt.

After waiting for a while, I pull out my Pre Calc homework and work on a few problems while I levitate in the air. A few after school and evening joggers pass by, and I ignore them as they snap photos of gawk at me.

"Holy cow! There's Superhero Chaos!" A little boy exclaims. I look up only to flash him a quick smile. It makes the kid's day, and the mother smiles at me. Yay. I have a fan base with a four-year-old and his mom now. Thrilling.

When they leave I sigh, uncrossing my legs and letting my feet fall to the ground. It's obvious that Phantom is busy with something else in his life since he always comes to the corn to play when he's bored. It's the only place that he shows up, and the only time Phantom is ever predictable. We both know it, and I think he likes to think of the field as out 'romantic meeting place' but our meeting here have never been romantic. Unless you count the time where he punched me through one floor of the school building because apparently he had a bad day and I pissed him off even more.

I put on my backpack and walk out of the field since the sun has begun to go down. Mrs. Henderson is probably worried about me and so is Anna. I take the busiest sidewalks to interfere with three would-be car accidents. There was my heroic deed for the day, and the news channel didn't even get a single glimpse. Good, I always hate the reporters and the cameramen. Fame is definitely not the reason why a person should become a superhero.

There is a person smoking a cigarette and I feel my blood run ice cold. My parents would give me cigarettes when I was in middle school. Mrs. Henderson had the hardest time killing that habit. It was the main reason why I couldn't live with Anna before Chaos jailed them. I cut off my breathing and count how long until the want passes. Twenty-two, twenty-three, twenty-four... There. My parents also could have given me drugs, since they were deep in that business, but I try not to think about that, never try to remember so I don't have to lie. But that's the life a lot of people downtown face. That's why crime is so rampant in the city. There's no middle class, just the wealthy and the poor.

I hustle and before I know it, I can't hold my breath any longer. I exhale, and quickly gulp in oxygen. The feeling of being a complete idiot washes over me. Waiting for Phantom to show up was just stupid. He is the most unpredictable being on the face of the Earth, so like he would show up when I waited for him.

There's the sound of tires squealing and I look up in time to see a van of grown men speeding way too fast. It was a scene out of a movie since there were pedestrians in the middle of the street who paused to squeal out my presence.

I run as fast as I can and jump on the side of the van, twenty feet away is the crosswalk, and my sneakers fumble for grip on the car. I go intangible, making the car and everyone and thing inside of it go through the mass of people. My heart pounds through my rib cage. There is a mountain of money bags in the back of the van. I go through the back of it, the driver swerving around because he knows that I am going to stop him. Sure enough, the whole back of the van was loaded with piles of cash. One hundred dollar bills were sloshing everywhere as the van moves. A man dons his mask and opens the small window that separated us. He points a gun at me, and I flinch. It's a small pistol, but I'm at the close range.

"Aye! It's Chaos!" the man cries, eyes wide.

"I was in the neighborhood," I shrug and look bored.

"She looks like a hobo in that sweatshirt. I thought you had class?" another man asks. He's stupid and didn't put on his ski mask.

I raise an eyebrow, "Well, I was desperate. Desperate times call for desperate measures."

"Get her out of here!" the driver calls out to his accomplices.

The man with the gun aims for my head, and I narrow my eyes, prepping myself for when he decides to press the trigger. To my surprise, the guy next to him throws a dagger at my neck. I go intangible and invisible, a small gasp escaping my lips. The three men laugh at me, which puts me in a bad mood.

I go through the middleman, and through the dash, pulling out random bits of the van's engine. A fire erupts and engulfs me, but I don't feel it. The driver swears at me, not helping my mood, but I step away from the van as the flames lick the engine. Luckily, people weren't around on this obscure street. I turn on my heel and, now fully visible but not tangible, walk away from the scene.

Now I had to find my way back to Anna's house, which I had no idea where I was taken. The sun dips closer to the horizon and I pull my phone out of my backpack and use the GPS to figure everything out. There are three missed texts from Anna saying how I'm lucky her parents are having a dinner with the Cardinale's and how I wasn't invited since I wasn't home, and the next was how boring the dinner was.

I smile and laugh. It is always good to see Anna suffering a little bit. The men run out of the doors of the van and I can hear their swearing as they watch helplessly at the van. They're too close to the car, and at any moment the van will explode.

As I turn the corner to the next street, I hear a huge KA-BOOM, and the men's laughter cuts off. I look back to see the three men splayed out on the asphalt, either dead but most likely unconscious. I flip my platinum blonde hair off my shoulders and continue walking. Serves them right for stealing.

Anna peers over me, her brown eyes wide and bright, "Kells? You okay?" she asks so innocently. The fact that I am laying on the kitchen's white tiled floor with a small, empty tub of Ben and Jerry's just out of reach from my fingertips should make it crystal clear that I was, in fact, not okay, but Anna asked the question anyway.

My green eyes slice into hers, "What do you think?" I asked, my voice sharp.

She jolts back, "Whoa, you looked like Phantom for a second," she gasps. I turn my head in my arms, staring at the tile floor.

"She's been here for over a half an hour," one of the cooks say. I don't know all of their names since the Hendersons switch cooks each month or whenever they want.

"How many Ben & Jerry's?" Anna inquired, her sock covered toe nudging my side.

"Just one, but she begged for more," the cook answered with a small laugh.

"Okay, she is definitely not okay. I'll get her downstairs, you can go back to whatever you were doing before," she tells the cook.

Her arms wrap around my middle and she heaves me up. I lean heavily against her, not wanting to walk or even stand.

I am dragged to the stairs before Anna threatens my life, "Either you walk downstairs by yourself or I push you down."

Since it was life or death, I choose to walk down the stairs by myself, listening to Anna's soft panting from carrying me. I wasn't that heavy for her to be panting so dang hard.

"You suck Capri Suns," Anna drops into the couch, pulling me next to her.

"I can live with that," I retort.

"What happened? You left me at school do work on math, making me do my own homework by myself, and then come home but die in the kitchen. Why?"

I wonder whether or not to tell Anna the truth that I was trying to get Phantom's attention and utterly failed at it. "Mmmm, do I have to answer that question? Cuz, I really don't feel like it."

She huffs angrily as I stuff a pillow to my face. Anna doesn't need to know why I am a blob of Jell-O because then it would involve why I wanted to meet Phantom. The last thing I need Anna to think was that we had a romantic rendezvous or something equally horrific. Heaven forbid!

"We were talking in English today that pineapple juice works great before getting wisdom teeth out. I wish we had known that. Pineapple juice is supposed to help the swelling go down, and I looked like an obese chipmunk!" Anna cries.

I almost laugh at the memory. Almost. Barely holding the laugh in. I was far better off than she was, since we got our wisdom teeth out the same day. Phantom and his gang decided to take the opportunity to set up the Mafia with police weapons, but that was the way life is for superheroes. When we aren't there, criminals run rampant. How many times have I put Phantom in jail? At least seventeen times, if not more. And he had put me in jail four times. Just four since it was a 'bother' to him.

"You're a cute chipmunk," I state. It's true when Anigirl ever chooses to be a chipmunk, which is twice in her lifetime. I may have teased her too much about it, and she refused to change into a chipmunk ever since. If needed, Anigirl changes into a squirrel or another animal that can get up a tree trunk.

Anna frowns, remembering my taunts. "Seriously? I thought we were over this, you really hurt my feelings." Her lips part into a pout, which looks childish on her. She is a totally girly girl, master of the duck face in her selfies, and always surrounded by people at lunch that she doesn't even know the names of. One could say that she was the most popular person at school. On the other hand, there was me. I was the type of girl who lived in the library, avoided any social interactions of every kind, and focused on schoolwork.

"Sorry about that," I say in a feeble attempt to patch things up. Anna sighs, and mumbles that she was going to go to her room and listen to the radio. I let her go,

Staring up at the ceiling, I start to worry about Anna. It seems like everything I do is worrying about my best friend and sister. At this rate, I was going to get gray hair! But Phantom didn't meet me at the cornfields, and that irritated me to no end.

I sigh and push myself off the couch to head back up the stairs. There's nobody awake, or even in the house, so I flip off all the lights in the kitchen after swiping a granola bar. The back of my neck tingles, and I know that Phantom is somewhere close by. Too bad he never shows up when I want him to.

I pretend not to notice because Phantom doesn't deserve my attention since I made it completely obvious that I needed to chat with him, and he ditched me. In a field. Of corn.

So that lame-O move did fit in with the 'What Would Phantom Do?' category. But that didn't make it any better.

I hear Anna shuffling in her room, and flip on the T.V., sitting up on the couch. When I did, my leg brushed something that felt like I knee. I jerk away, eyeing the place on the couch suspiciously. "What on Earth?" I ask.

Suddenly, there's pressure over my mouth, and Phantom appears right in front of me, crouching on the floor by my feet. Of course, I scream, totally not expecting him to touch me, but his gloved hand muffles it over my mouth.

"Don't move a muscle," He says softly so Anna wouldn't hear in her room.

I freeze, eyes widening. Why would Phantom show up when I didn't want him to show up? I waited in that dang corn field for hours and yet when I finally resigned myself to not getting any answers, he poofs out of nowhere! What was a girl supposed to do?

"Kelsey, correct?" he asks, not wanting a reply because we both knew that it was right. "Well, Kelsey, let me tell you a secret. May I?" he asks, leaning his face towards mine.

"S-sure. Go ahead and spill," I say, slightly intimidated.

"Your friend Anna is in deep doo-doo and if you want to be caught up in all that danger then keep hanging out with herrrrr..." He holds the 'R' and a smirk creeps on his face.

"What danger?" I ask, narrowing my eyes.

"Let's just say that a lot of people do not like her," he replies ever so cryptic.

I imagine banging my head against the sharpest corner I could find. He wasn't telling me anything new, but maybe I could find some answers. What ever that case, if he tells me, then that would be fantastic, even if the last thing he would do is tell Kelsey anything.

"Well, why don't you go ask Chaos for help of something? Don't you like her?" I ask, scooting away from him as slyly as possible.

"Because Chaos wants to know things that I don't want to tell her," he says, wagging a gloved finger and tsking at me, "I would suggest you stop with your questions I know you have. Yes, I'll kiss you before I leave, no I won't take a selfie with you or sign the giant poster you have hanging in your room," he states.

My jaw drops to the floor, "You went in my room?" I screech. Yeah, my room did have a giant Phantom poster on the ceiling above my bed, but trust me- the poster is only there for me to throw darts at. Anna gave me the idea to put it on a giant cork board that was in the garage so I can vent out all my frustration.

"I must say, the dart holes are not becoming, although you haven't hit my head, thank you very much," he smirks at me and sits on the couch.

"Just everywhere else on your body," I finish.

The thought of Phantom of all people going in my room made me feel nervous. I narrow my eyes at him, and he does the same to me. For a moment his eyes widen though and he starts to laugh. The noise is like a fingernail scraping against a cheese grater. Not good.

Before thinking, I cover his mouth with my hand, "Shut up! Anna is in her room!" I hiss.

His face goes through my hand, which makes my hand tingle like it's asleep, "Can I trust that Anna is safe in your care? We look so much alike, Miss Kelsey, it's uncanny," he notes.

Not good, not good, not good! Abort mission ASAP! my mind chimes.

"Anna's safe with me, I promise. Plus, I think every boy who has black hair and green eyes look like you. You can't possibly tell me you dress like that all day long," I cover, motioning to his black slacks and black button down that has the sleeves rolled up to the elbows and a silver tie.

"I must admit that I don't dress like this all day long. Sometimes in the morning, I wear a sweater because it's so darn cold outside it makes me think about throwing sharp objects around at innocent bystanders," he smiles innocently at me.

I think about how to respond without saying Yeah, let's not throw sharp objects at innocent bystanders, shall we? like I desperately wanted to. That would be too witty, and although Kelsey was smart, she was not supposed to be witty. "I'm sorry you have issues with the cold. Maybe you should move to California?"

He muses over the thought, "I would love to, except for the fact that California already has twelve villains, and none of the heroes are as cute as Chaos. But maybe I'll visit," he says.

"Go for it. Okay, so now that you know Anna's safe, can't you leave?" I ask politely.

"Why? You don't like me?" he asks, pretending to be hurt.

"If the poster dart board wasn't a hint, then you must be dense," I mutter under my breath. He hears it and chuckles.

"Maybe this will change your mind?" he leans in close to me. Sirens wail in my head, but this is normal for him. Phantom always kisses girls good-bye. This is no big.

But as his lips tauntingly brush over mine, my heart flutters. It's wrong, so wrong because the hero never falls in love with the villain. I definitely did not have any feelings for this psycho. Besides, it was normal for Phantom to kiss his fans goodbye, completely normal.

So my heart shouldn't have thudded like a sledgehammer when he pulls back and then presses those lips full on to mine. Yet it totally does.

When Phantom kisses Chaos it was full of passion, yet gentle at the same time. Yeah, he's kissed Chaos- me- before. With a few years of kicking his trashy butt around town, a girl earns a few Phantom kisses. Yet, when he kissed me as Kelsey, there was nothing. No feelings, just a tease.

So when he pulls back and then disappeared into nowhere, a part of me feels hallow. Not cool. My fingers come up to my lips, and I bit my bottom lip. There wasn't a trace of Phantom's pungent spice on my lips like usual.

I groan, laying back quickly so my head flops onto the couch cushions and bounces, "Stupid Phantom. Stupid secrets, stupid kiss, stupid Phantom's face, stupid psycho killer person," I chant to the ceiling. It's a feeble attempt to calm myself down that doesn't work.

Anna is in danger, I know that, but Phantom must be desperate if he told Kelsey that. The danger definitely must be bigger than I had originally thought.

Thinking about this, I don't notice Anna open the door to her room and walk to the bathroom. Only when she turns the water on that I notice.

Crap! I am the worst protector ever! I cry in my mind, propping myself up. "Anna, are you going to bed?"

She comes out, toothbrush in her mouth, "Mmm."

My eyebrows furrow as I try to decide in the 'mmm' was a yes or no. Deciding it is most likely a yes I stand up, "Me too."

I get up and walk to my room, the room Phantom came into. A shiver passes through my body, but nothing looks touched or out of place. Why would he come in here? I ask myself. There wasn't an answer, so I get fresh pajamas out of the dresser, and continue getting ready for bed.

Chapter 4

Last night I was doing Pre Calc homework, working with notation crap, outside Mr. and Mrs. Hederson's room in their little 'waiting area' with a front room set of plushy couches, and a coffee table. Nobody was home except for me and Anna- my partner in crime (sometimes literally) who was in our 'secret lair' of the house's basement supposedly working on her vocabulary flash cards. Right after school we worked on her math, so at least that was already finished. But while I was dazing in between intricate math problems in the silence when I heard Anna shriek so loudly, even I could hear it.

I started, standing up so fast, that the text book and papers fell on my feet, making me cry out in pain. That textbook was heavy!

I limped down the spiral staircase down to the basement, where Anna was running and Superman-ed face first on the couch.

Raising an eyebrow I asked, "Anna, I know this is a basement, but the couch is not first base so what happened?"

She laughed, "Stop being so weird, saying stuff like that. Does the basement look like a baseball diamond?"

That retort made me smile widely, "I don't know, you're the one sliding around."

"Suck it!" she hissed. I knew that she wouldn't answer my question about what happened, because of her sour attitude. Anna never has a sour attitude unless it was the last week of the month, when her period started and she had major cramps.

"O...kay? Who peed in your Cheerios?" I stuck out my tongue at her and slowly backed away.

"KELSEY IMMA KIIIIILLL YOU!" she literally roared at me.

I placed a hand over my hear and took a deep breath like I had gotten impaled, "Ohmawerd! Someone save me from Anna's animalistic wrath! I swear I didn't tinkle in her Cheerios! Anna doesn't even like Cheerios!" I cried while grasping the staircase and running up it.

I stopped when I realized that she wasn't following me.

Only later did Anna tell me that Phantom was in the basement, and he popped out of nowhere which was why she screamed. Apparently he was just 'checking up on pretty ladies' which was a lie. He probably couldn't handle being invisible for any longer, which only happened to Phantom once every... oh, every five years or so. But to me, it happened all the flippin' time.

Now I was sleeping in my English class when we were supposed to read a chapter of the class's book that I had previously read. The academy, with an obscure name of someone who had a seriously strange spelling to their last name, required a uniform with a long black skirt that wasn't pleated- thank goodness, and a white button down shirt with a gray vest or coat. Vests make my armpits hurt, so I gave all of mine to Anna, who says that sweater vests make her look smarter in a non-nerd related way... whatever that meant.

"Nice of you to join room 410, Miss Jerrs," the teacher looked over her half moon glasses at me.

"Ah, sorry," I apologized, hurrying to open the book as fast as possible and pretending to read it.

"King Macbeth is insane!" a girl stage whispered next to me, looking at the other girl on the other side of me. Great, everyday these two girls talk while I am stuck between them. Talk about boring.

"I know! He kind of reminds me of one of your boyfriends. Remember John?" Girl 2 asked.

Girl 1 gasped, "Oh my, yeah! Yeah, he's totally Macbeth crazy!"

Honey, you do not understand the play if you think King Macbeth is like your boyfriend, I want to jump in, but I didn't.

"And his wife is like Marley Fern!" Girl 1 added. Who on earth was Marley Fern? Was she manipulative and greedy?

"Ew. I totally hate that Fern girl," Girl 2 makes a face.

And I was in the middle of them. Always excluded, yet always in the middle of things that I don't want to deal with.

Fern... Did I know a girl with the last name of Fern? The name sounds a bit familiar.

Personally, I thought that the king and his wife were a lot like my parents. Killing people for their gain and stuff like that. It was one of the reasons I took the book home to read it through, even if I did not read a single book all my high school life before, let alone Shakespeare.

A girl could only hope that the dead people haunted her parents while they were in the maximum security prison.

Is that a strange thought? If Anna heard me say something like that she'd give me a serious tongue lashing saying things like, "Kelsey! They are your parents, and you love them! Don't think otherwise! I don't care if they've murdered hundreds of teenagers nationwide to get drugs! They're getting over their addictions anyways!"

And that is the last thing I needed in my life.

"Emerald Cardinale looked at me today!" Girl 1 whispers a little bit quieter.

Ah, they always bring up that boy. He doesn't attend this academy- I don't even think he goes to school. How old was he? Anyways, Emerald and Girl 1 lived by each other, although that could mean that he lived five blocks away from her, but I don't care how close he really lived because that would be useless information.

"No way! That's the third time this week!"

"Yeah, I swear he likes me!"

"Girl, I have to sleep over on Friday so I could see him too!" Girl 2 squealed.

"Miss Backett, Jerrs, and Hardy. Must I tell you three to be quiet and read again or will you just do whatever you're supposed to do for once in your lives?" the teacher asks. I really despised her funky half moon glasses. Why did she wear glasses if she was looking over them all the dang time?

And of course, my last name was grouped with the two who really were talking even though I didn't say a peep. How frustrating.

I huff under my breath, and bury my nose in the play. This hour should have been spent by me sleeping away quietly right next to Miss Benson's desk. I always slept on reading days, since I finished that book in three days. What was the interesting part was when Miss Benson would dive so deeply and intimately into the plot, or the reasons the characters acted the way they did, why Macbeth had to kill his friend. That was the reason why I was here.

Girl 1 and 2 went back to reading, smiles on their faces as they thought about Emerald rather than the play.

Emerald Cardinale's family was extremely rich. I knew that Miss Benson was secretly dating the oldest brother named Hayden. There were five boys, age thirty-one to twelve- Hayden, Jonah, Noah, Mark, and then little Brigg. They were the third richest family in the world, and had a mansion that was even bigger than the Henderson's. I've gone to their lavish Christmas parties they threw each year, and that's how I knew that Miss Benson was hitting on Hayden.

They made a super cute couple. Miss Benson was in her mid-twenties so Hayden wasn't too old for her. Whenever the couple had a date, the whole school could tell and my class usually weaseled the facts from her with as much detail as possible.

When the bell to leave class finally rings, I hadn't even turned the page of the book that I've been staring at blankly.

I gather my belongings, holding the book in my arms like the nerds did because my backpack is already zipped shut so what was the point of putting the book in it when the next class-Pre Calc- is just in the other building?

A smile creeps on my face when I realize that it was my absolute favorite class of the day. Math is easy, math is fun, math is my entire world. What can a person do with math? Everything.

Practically skipping to my next class, I catch myself thinking about what Phantom had said that one night in the warehouse. How I can't afford to slip up as Chaos or as Kelsey. I had slipped up big time last night, not noticing that Phantom was in the room. Usually I could feel his energy but last night I didn't. That scared me big time. Was I being sloppy? Anna's well-being cannot afford my sloppiness.

I slip behind my desk and put my elbows on the table, fingers grasping my black hair. Mr. Monroe wasn't in the classroom and there wouldn't be the class until a few seconds after the tardy bell.

Everything is so hard. The danger that loomed beyond the horizon scared me since Phantom made me aware of it. Could Anna tell that something big was being planned? And then there was the fact that everyday villains like Gorilla man that I wasn't sure was part of Phantom's circle or not. Those villains never committed serious crimes, never had enough power to even try half the things Phantom did every night.

I needed to talk to him tonight no matter what. I needed to evade Anna and somehow find that elusive man. How am I supposed to find someone who is literally a phantom when they don't want to be found? I mean, he's the one that shows up whenever he wants to torment me.

Plus, I had to endure the school life before I could do any sleuthing or find any clues to my questions. Of course, Phantom wouldn't give me a straightforward answer, but at least it was something rather than nothing.

Mr. Monroe stands at the front of the room and began to speak. I attempted to listen as he handed out the new monthly homework calendars. Those calendars were the only reason I wasn't failing the class. By doing as much Pre Calc as I could on the nights that I had time to do homework meant that I taught myself all the precepts that Mr. Monroe was babbling about.

And Anna's mom wonders why I didn't take a college course. There isn't any time for me to fit in High School and College. Rarely, very rarely, did I have time to relax and take a nap after I finished my homework and house chores. (Mrs. Henderson doesn't let the maid clean downstairs so we can 'learn' to clean up after ourselves.)

We get our homework with fifteen minutes left in class. Mr. Monroe likes to give us at least some time at the end of class to start on it, so we can ask questions or discuss what we don't really understand. I work furiously until the bell rang.

Then finally, I was free to go. I almost cry as I scurry off campus, sending a quick text to Anna telling her not to wait for me. Phantom knows everything, and I needed his answers right away. He has to be home, since the public and the private school was out of session now- if he even is a high school student, which I'm not sure.

Practically running down the sidewalk to get to the corn fields at the back of the school, I slow down. There is no need to look suspicious.

It's chilly, so rather than change with a dew stalks of corn to cover me, I just slip on a black hoodie and call it good with black ankle boots which were all in my backpack. (I know, those items take up a lot of space!)

I let out a long sigh, hoping that I can find Phantom. If he isn't out tonight then I didn't know what I would do. Maybe I'll save a few robberies or stop car crashes on the main street like I used to do before Phantom sauntered into my freaking life.

Before Anna was in deep doo-doo.

I run my fingers through my long white hair. It's pretty silky because of Anna's shampoo expertise. She gets this exotic blend of many spices and fruit that supposedly are really good for hair. Whatever.

Being Chaos is always amusing to me. Sometimes, people won't notice who I am until I use my superpowers or some-times people freak out and go all fangirl over me, begging me to touch them or sign their arm or something odd. Anna loves her fans, she has perfected her Anigirl signature to look like a paw print, and not even close to her real handwriting. Phantom is amazing with his fans, although he'd rather die than let those people touch him. He just goes through them when they get in his way. Rush likes to joke around with his fans. Me? Well I just smile and wave, avoiding contact and not answering reporter's questions. I believe that there's a meme of me that's all "this is what silence looks like" with my face. Oh well, what can a girl do?

The itchy corn brushes on my sweatshirt, making it messy with the dust and dirt that are on the leaves. I try patting my shirt clean, but it only makes it worse. Phantom loves the corn fields so I'm hoping that he will take a mid afternoon stroll.

Letting my feet levitate off the floor, I rise above the field, hoping to get attention from a certain someone.

I put up my guard, waiting for Phantom's sharp voice to say something like "Don't you look like poo today," or something. But of course, there isn't any sign of him. How annoying. But standing in the silence with nothing to better me except the corn stalks brushing against my sweatshirt.

After waiting for a while, I pull out my PreCalc homework and work on a few problems while I levitate in the air. A few after school and evening joggers pass by, and I ignore them as they snap photos of me and gawk.

"Holy cow! There's Superhero Chaos!" A little boy exclaims. I look up only to flash him a quick smile. It makes the kid's day, and the mother smiles at me. Yay. I have a fan base with a four year old and his mom now. Thrilling.

When they leave I sigh, uncrossing my legs and letting my feet fall to the ground. It's obvious that Phantom is busy with something else in his life since he always comes to the corn to play when he's bored. It's the only place that he shows up, and the only time Phantom is ever predictable. We both know it,and I think he likes to think of the field as out 'romantic meeting place' but our meeting here have never been romantic. Unless you count the time where he punched me through one floor of the school building because apparently he had a bad day and I pissed him off even more.

I put on my backpack and walk out of the field since the sun has begun to go down. Mrs. Henderson is probably worries about me and so is Anna. I take the busiest sidewalks to interfere with three would-be car accidents. There was my heroic deeds for the day, and the news channel didn't even get a single glimpse. Good, I always hate the reporters and the cameramen. Fame is definitely not the reason why a person should become a superhero.

There is a person smoking on a cigarette and I feel my blood run ice cold. My parents would give me cigarettes when I was in middle school. Mrs. Henderson had the hardest time killing that habit. It was the main reason why I couldn't live with Anna before Chaos jailed them. I cut off my breathing and count how long until the want passes. Twenty-two, twenty-three, twenty-four... There. My parents also could have given me drugs, since they were deep in that business, but I try not to think about that, never try to remember so I don't have to lie. But that's the life a lot of people downtown face. That's why crime is so rampant in the city. There's not middle class, just the wealthy and the poor.

I hustle and before I know it, I can't hold my breath any longer. I exhale, and quickly gulp in oxygen. The feeling of being a complete idiot washes over me. Waiting for Phantom to show up was just stupid. He is the most unpredictable being on the face of the Earth, so like he would show up when I waited for him.

There's the sound of tires squealing and I look up in time to see a van of grown men speeding way too fast. It was a scene out of a movie, since there were pedestrians in the middle of the street who paused to squeal out my presence.

I run as fast as I can and jump on the side of the van, twenty feet away is the crosswalk, and my sneakers fumble for grip on the car. I go intangible, making the car and everyone and thing inside of it go through the mass of people. My heart pounds through my rib cage. There is a mountain of money bags in the back of the van. I go through the back of it, the driver swerving around because he knows that I am going to stop him. Sure enough, the whole back of the van was loaded with piles of cash. One hundred dollar bills were sloshing everywhere as the van moves. A man dons on his mask, and opens the small window that separated us. He points a gun at me, and I flinch. It's a small pistol, but I'm at close range.

"Aye! It's Chaos!" the man cries, eyes wide.

"I was in the neighborhood," I shrug and look bored.

"She looks like a hobo in that sweatshirt. I thought you had class?" another man asks. He's stupid and didn't put on his ski mask.

I raise an eyebrow, "Well, I was desperate. Desperate times call for desperate measures."

"Get her out of here!" the driver calls out to his accomplices.

The man with the gun aims for my head, and I narrow my eyes, prepping myself for when he decides to press the trigger. To my surprise, the guy next to him throws a dagger at my neck. I go intangible and invisible, a small gasp escaping my lips. The three men laugh at me, which puts me in a bad mood.

I go through the middle man, and through the dash, pulling out random bits of the van's engine. A fire erupts and engulfs me, but I don't feel it. The driver swears at me, not helping my mood, but I step away from the van as the flames lick the engine. Luckily, people weren't around on this obscure street. I turn on my heel and, now fully visible but not tangible, walk away from the scene.

Now I had to find my way back to Anna's house, which I had no idea where I was taken. The sun dips closer to the horizon and I pull my phone out of my backpack and use the GPS to figure everything out. There's three missed texts from Anna saying how I'm lucky her parents are having a dinner with the Cardinale's and how I wasn't invited since I wasn't home, and the next were how boring the dinner was.

I smile and laugh. It is always good to see Anna suffering a little bit. The men run out of the doors of the van and I can hear their swearing as they watch helplessly at the van. They're too close to the car, and at any moment the van will explode.

As I turn the corner to the next street, I hear a huge KA-BOOM, and the men's laughter cuts off. I look back to see the three men splayed out on the asphalt, either dead but most likely unconscious. I flip my platinum blonde hair off my shoulders and continue walking. Serves them right for stealing.

Chapter 5

Anna peers over me, her brown eyes wide and bright, "Kells? You okay?" she asks so innocently. The fact that I am laying on the kitchen's white tiled floor with a small, empty tub of Ben and Jerry's just out of reach from my fingertips should make it crystal clear that I was, in fact, not okay, but Anna asked the question anyways.

My green eyes slice into hers, "What do you think?" I asked, my voice sharp.

She jolts back, "Whoa, you looked like Phantom for a second," she gasps. I turn my head in my arms, staring at the tile floor.

"She's been here for over a half an hour," one of the cooks say. I don't know all of their names since the Hendersons switch cooks each month or whenever they want.

"How many Ben & Jerry's?" Anna inquired, her sock covered toe nudging my side.

"Just one, but she begged for more," the cook answered with a small laugh.

"Okay, she is definitely not okay. I'll get her downstairs, you can go back to whatever you were doing before," she tells the cook.

Her arms wrap around my middle and she heaves me up. I lean heavily against her, not wanting to walk or even stand.

I am dragged to the stairs before Anna threatens my life, "Either you walk downstairs by yourself or I push you down."

Since it was life or death, I choose to walk down the stairs by myself, listening to Anna's soft panting from carrying me. I wasn't that heavy for her to be panting so dang hard.

"You suck Capri Suns," Anna drops into the couch, pulling me next to her.

"I can live with that," I retort.

"What happened? You left me at school do work on math, making me do my own homework by myself, and then come home but die in the kitchen. Why?"

I ponder whether or not to tell Anna the truth, that I was trying to get Phantom's attention and utterly failed at it. "Mmmm, do I have to answer that question? Cuz, I really don't feel like it."

She huffs angrily as I stuff a pillow to my face. Anna doesn't need to know why I am a blob of Jell-O because then it would involve why I wanted to meet Phantom. The last thing I need Anna to think was we had a romantic rendezvous or something equally horrific. Heaven forbid!

"We were talking in English today that pineapple juice works great before getting wisdom teeth out. I wish we had known that. Pineapple juice is supposed to help the swelling go down, and I looked like an obese chipmunk!" Anna cries.

I almost laugh at the memory. Almost. Barely holding the laugh in. I was far better off than she was, since we got our wisdom teeth out the same day. Phantom and his gang decided to take the opportunity to set up the Mafia with police weapons, but that was the way life is for superheros. When we aren't there, criminals run rampant. How many times have I put Phantom in jail? At least seventeen. And he had put me in jail four times. Just four since it was a 'bother' to him.

"You're a cute chipmunk," I state. It's true, when Anigirl ever chooses to be a chipmunk, which is twice in her lifetime. I may have teased her too much about it, and she refused to change into a chipmunk ever since. If needed, Anigirl changes into a squirrel or another animal that can get up a tree trunk.

Anna frowns, remembering my taunts. "Seriously? I thought we were over this, you really hurt my feelings." Her lips part into a pout, which looks cute one her. She is a totally girly girl, master of the duck face in her selfies, and always surrounded by people at lunch that she doesn't even know the names of. One could say that she was the most popular person at school. On the other hand, there was me. I was the type of girl who are in the library, avoided any social interactions of every kind, and focused on schoolwork.

"Sorry about that," I say in a feeble attempt to patch things up. Anna sighs, and mumbles that she was going to go to her room and listen to the radio. I let her go,

Staring up at the ceiling, I start to worry about Anna. It seems like everything I do is worrying about my best friend and sister. At this rate, I was going to get gray hair! But Phantom didn't meet me at the corn fields, and that irritated me to no end.

I sigh and push myself off the couch to head back up the stairs. There's nobody awake, or even in the house, so I flip off all the lights in the kitchen after swiping a granola bar. The back of my neck tingles, and I know that Phantom is somewhere close by. Too bad he never shows up when I want him to.

I pretend not to notice, because Phantom doesn't deserve my attention since I made it completely obvious that I needed to chat with him, and he ditched me. In a field. Of corn.

So that lame-O move did fit in with the 'What Would Phantom Do?' category. But that didn't make it any better.

I hear Anna shuffling in her room, and flip on the T.V., sitting up in the couch. When I did, my leg brushed something that felt like I knee. I jerk away, eyeing the place on the couch suspiciously. "What on Earth?" I ask.

Suddenly, there's pressure over my mouth, and Phantom appears right in front of me, crouching on the floor by my feet. Of course I scream, totally not expecting him to touch me, but it's muffled by his gloved hand over my mouth.

"Don't move a muscle," He says softly so Anna wouldn't hear in her room.

I freeze, eyes widening. Why would Phantom show up when I didn't want him to show up? I waited in that dang corn field for hours and yet when I finally resigned myself to not getting any answers, he poofs out of nowhere! What was a girl supposed to do?

"Kelsey, correct?" he asks, not wanting a reply, because we both knew that it ws right. "Well, Kelsey, let me tell you a secret. May I?" he asks, leaning his face towards mine.

"S-sure. Go ahead and spill," I say, slightly intimidated.

"Your friend Anna is in deep doo-doo and if you want to be caught up in all that danger then keep hanging out with herrrrr..." He holds the 'R' and a smirk creeps on his face.

"What danger?" I ask, narrowing my eyes.

"Let's just say that a lot of people do not like her," he replies ever so cryptic.

I imagine banging my head against the sharpest corner I could find. He wasn't telling me anything new, but maybe I could find some answers. What ever that case, if he tells me, then that would be fantastic, even if the last thing he would do is tell Kelsey anything.

"Well, why don't you go ask Chaos for help of something? Don't you like her?" I ask, scooting away from him as slyly as possible.

"Because Chaos wants to know things that I don't want to tell her," he says, wagging a gloved finger and tsking at me, "I would suggest you stop with your questions I know you have. Yes, I'll kiss you before I leave, no I won't take a selfie with you or sign the giant poster you have hanging in your room," he states.

My jaw drops to the floor, "You went in my room?" I screech. Yeah, my room did have a giant Phantom poster on the ceiling above my bed, but trust me- the poster is only there for me to throw darts at. Anna gave me the idea to put it on a giant cork board that was in the garage so I can vent out all my frustration.

"I must say, the dart holes are not becoming, although you haven't hit my head, thank you very much," he smirks at me, and sits on the couch.

"Just everywhere else on your body," I finish.

The thought of Phantom of all people going in my room made me feel nervous. I narrow my eyes at him, and he does the same to me. For a moment his eyes widen though and he starts to laugh. The noise is like a fingernail scraping against a cheese grater. Not good.

Before thinking, I cover his mouth with my hand, "Shut up! Anna is in her room!" I hiss.

His face goes through my hand, which makes my hand tingle like it's asleep, "Can I trust that Anna is safe in your care? We look so much alike, Miss Kelsey, it's uncanny," he notes.

Not good, not good, not good! Abort mission ASAP! my mind chimes.

"Anna's safe with me, I promise. Plus, I think every boy who has black hair and green eyes look like you. You can't possibly tell me you dress like that all day long," I cover, motioning to his black slacks and black button down that has the sleeves rolled up to the elbows, and a silver tie.

"I must admit that I don't dress like this all day long. Some-times in the morning, I wear a sweater because it's so darn cold outside it makes me think about throwing sharp ojects around at innocent bystanders," he smiles innocently at me.

I think about how to respond without saying Yeah, let's not throw sharp objects at innocent bystanders, shall we? like I desperately wanted to. That would be to witty, and although Kesley was smart, she was not supposed to be witty. "I'm sorry you have issues with the cold. Maybe you should move to California?"

He muses over the thought, "I would love to, except for the fact that California already has twelve villains, and none of the heroes are as cute as Chaos. But maybe I'll visit," he says.

"Go for it. Okay, so now that you know Anna's safe, can't you leave?" I ask politely.

"Why? You don't like me?" he asks, pretending to be hurt.

"If the poster dart board wasn't a hint, then you must be dense," I mutter under my breath. He hears it and chuckles.

"Maybe this will change you mind?" he leans in close to me. Sirens wail in my head, but this is normal for him. Phantom always kisses girls good-bye. This is no big.

But as his lips tauntingly brush over mine, my heart flutters. It's wrong, so wrong, because the hero never falls in love with the villain. I definitely did not have any feelings for this psycho. Besides, it was normal for Phantom to kiss his fans goodbye, completely normal.

So my heart shouldn't have thudded like a sledgehammer when he pulled back, and then pressed those lips full on to mine. Yet it totally did.

When Phantom kisses Chaos it was full of passion, yet gentle at the same time. Yeah, he's kissed Chaos- me- before. With a few years of kicking his trashy butt around town, a girl earns a few Phantom kisses. Yet, when he kissed me as Kelsey, there was nothing. No feelings, just a tease.

So when he pulled back, and then disappeared into nowhere, a part of me felt hallow. Not cool. My fingers come up to my lips, and I bit my bottom lip. There wasn't a trace of Phantom's pungent spice on my lips like usual.

I groan, laying back quickly so my head flops onto the couch cushions and bounces, "Stupid Phantom. Stupid secrets, stupid kiss, stupid Phantom's face, stupid psycho killer person," I chant to the ceiling. It's a feeble attempt to calm myself down that doesn't work.

Anna is in danger, I know that, but Phantom must be desperate if he told Kelsey that. The danger definitely must be bigger than I had originally thought.

Thinking about this, I don't notice Anna open the door to her room and walk to the bathroom. Only when she turns the water on that I notice.

Crap! I am the worst protector ever! I cry in my mind, propping myself up. "Anna, are you going to bed?"

She comes out, toothbrush in her mouth, "Mmm."

My eyebrows furrow as I try to decide in the 'mmm' was a yes or no. Deciding it is most likely a yes I stand up, "Me too."

I get up and walk to my room, the room Phantom came into. A shiver passes through my body, but nothing looks touched or out of place. Why would he come in here? I ask myself. There wasn't an answer, so I get fresh pajamas out of the dresser, and continue getting ready for bed.

Chapter 6

Once school got out on a Tuesday evening, I decided to head into town rather than go home with Anna. Anna was as normal as ever, surrounded by hundreds of people and smiling like always. On the other hand, I was a nervous wreck. Math problems kept running in my head like a movie reel loop and in English I didn't do a single question on the Romeo and Juliet packet we received in preparation for the book's test.

I figure going into town and checking out some of my favorite shops and little boutiques would be a nice stress reliever. After all, I needed to go into the little Wiccan shop and get a few crystal necklaces. Amazonite and blue Quartz would definitely help me calm down- at least that's what the little Wiccan Meaning of Crystals Chart said. I got a small Amazonite stone and a medium sized blue Quartz that was wrapped in wire.

"You have a chain?" the woman at the counter asks me. There is an array of different length chains to my left but I don't mind them.

"Yeah I do at home," I reply politely.

She nods, and eyes the small Onyx crystal that dangles off of one of my many bracelets. Onyx is the main reason I come here. Apparently, the stone repelled negativity and can 'create invisibility' by absence of light. Heaven knows I needed something to repel all of Phantom's negativity. That man will kill me with how pessimistic he's been recently. Phantom has been whiny and extra clingy, not to mention that for the first time in my life there are deep purple circles underneath his eyes from lack of sleep.

I walk out of the shop with the small bag in hand. There are people hustling about to and fro and I watch them like the stalker I deny being. It's a usual Tuesday evening and not a lot of people are around. Young moms push their baby strollers on the sidewalk as their shopping bags hang off the handles. I protect these people from harm. There are people that like to hurt others, people that are worse than Phantom could ever dream to be.

...Speaking of the devil...

He saunters towards me, but on the opposite side of the street. I duck my head down, pretening to run my fingers over the stones like they were the center of my universe. Please don't let Phantom see me, please, please, please! I chant in my head.

But I know Phantom is too busy checking himself out in the shop's window out of the corner of his eye to notice much of anything surrounding him.

I slip into an empty clothing store. Immediately I am bombarded by a girl my age.

"Looking for the perfect prom dress?" she asks and I realize that it is a formal wear shop. Shoot.

"Uh- actually no. No! I mean yes. Yes, I am looking for a dress, but not for prom," I stumble over my words. Everyone says that I am a terrible on the spot liar. Hopefully the girl doesn't notice that trait. I eye her careful just to make sure that she doesn't get that I'm lying. Was the school prom even close? Second semester hadn't even started!

The girl stares at me very deeply, "You look like Phantom," she states. My heart nearly beats out of my chest.

"No I do not! I'm just me. Not Phantom!" I say quickly. Then I rethink what I just said and then fix it, "Sorry, I actually get that a lot. Everyone says that we look alike, but in reality it's just that hair and eyes that are similar."

"And your attitudes," the girl scoffs.

That surprises me, "Our attitudes?" I mimic stupidly.

"So, I'm guessing you want a black dress?" she evades my question. I frown, beginning to be ticked off.

"No, I would like to look around first. BTW, Phantom is outside roaming the streets. You can look, don't worry, I won't steal anything," I tell her.

The girl's eyes widen like saucers, "Phantom is here?" she squeals excitedly and runs to the shop's front windows to peer outside.

From her scream, I assumed that she saw him. I look around at the dresses and notice an older man behind the cash register staring me down. Why would a man work at a dress shop? I eye him suspiciously back, since he is glaring at me.

Rude much?

When the man looks to the young woman in the front window, I yank a random dress off the rack and hustle into the changing rooms to 'try it on'. Inside the changing room, I turn invisible and yank off my backpack and pull out Chaos's outfit, stripping off my own. I feel my hair shorten and the tingle of my scalp indicates the color changing to white blonde. Hopefully the man over the counter wouldn't miss me. I slip the rocks into the side of my backpack.

I slide under the door, thankful that the door wasn't all the way down to the tile so I can slide through without using my powers and alerting Phantom. I could get away with invisibility, but phasing through walls requires much more power and effort making it easier for us to sense each other when we use it.

When I get to the entrance of the building I look to see where Phantom is. He has stopped to watch a tall skyscraper intently. That only means one thing- it was going to explode.

I run through the door, and Phantom's head turns to my direction. As soon as I am far enough away from the shop I left I turn visible and slam into Phantom's body.

Not a good Idea, his body is rock solid muscle. I bounce back like a bouncy ball.

"Just the girl I was hoping to see," Phantom says menac-ingly. His green eyes narrow at me, ans his lips twitch into a smirk, "You got here fast. I haven't even blown up the bank's vaults. Of course it's not like I need extra cash. It's just fun-something you don't seem to understand..." he trails off at the end.

I glare at him for insulting me, "Wow, who peed in you Cherrios today? Pissy much?"

"Well, Rush did force me to go to this awful villain meeting. Don't worry, the cops attempted to break it up. They're dead now but if you'd like to know the location of their bodies I could tell you... or not?" he snickers evillyy.

"You're messed up in the head. I suggest therapy," I state seriously.

Phantom pokes his tongue at me, flashing a tongue pierc-ing. Rather than reply to my comment, he turns his attention to the building, "Tick tick boom."

There's a loud BOOM! as the explosives go off. People scream, and my blood freezes in my veins.

Phantom laughs maniacally at me, "I blew up people and you let me. Naughty, naughty. Chaos is such a naughty hero."

I stare, frozen in place. How many people died because I didn't save them in time? I am utterly horrified at myself, and he takes the opportunity, to wrap his arms around me and we sink into the earth.

There is no feasible way I can move after that. I just stare at Phantom in shock. It's been months since the last time he killed innocent people. His style is more capture, threaten then release.

"Poor Chaos. You did surprise me, I assumed that you would take care of the bomb before you talked to me. Do I worry you that much with the news of Anigirl? You're safe in my arms now," he says soothingly. His gloved fingers trail up and down my arms in what is supposed to be a soothing gesture, but it's anything but soothing.

I shiver violently against his chest, and Phantom grins. He begins to walk to the left, taking me somewhere he doesn't want me to see. It is uncanny how one could walk underground in complete darkness and know where he is and how to get where he wants to go. Phantom coos that with practice, I could do that also.

"You're vile," I hiss, angry at him for hurting others.

"Aren't all villains 'vile' though?" Phantom counters. He is unrepentant like always.

"Just because you woke up on the wrong side of the bed does not mean it is okay to blow people up in a bank!" I yell, trying to get free of his arms. If he does let go, I'll be completely lost underground, and it could take hours for me to figure out which was is up.

Phantom pulls me so I have hanging over his shoulders. His arm wraps around the bottom hem of my black silk skirt, and my gray shirt rides up. I can feel Phantom's gloves on the bare skin of my back, and I blush. Such an awkward position to be in with this person.

"Feisty, I like it," he states as I try to kick him in the sweet spot. Even if I did land a kick where I want to, he had a cup to shield that area so it wouldn't hurt him.

"And I don't like that you're angry!"

He changes direction and muses on his reply for a second, "We all give and we take. I'm a villain. By law, villains kill people. We don't have to be Joker wanna-be's, but we kill people. If the group thinks I'm soft, then I will show them that I am not soft in order to protect you."

Finally, we arrive in a dark room. I can tell it's not underground anymore, because our bodies solidify and there's a tinkling of a ceiling fan. Red numbers on the alarm clock read that it's seven in the evening, and I assume the alarm clock is on a nightstand, not that I can see it clearly.

It's his secret hideout, I realize with a start as he drops me on the bed. Why would Phantom bring me here?

There's a click, and then the bedside lights up from a small lamp. Phantom's eyes pierce mine, "So, why have you been calling me everyday this week?" he asks.

"You heard me?" I counter flatly. My fists clench together tightly and I fume silently at him.

"Yeah, but I'm busy and completely ignored you. So what?" he shrugs like it's no big deal.

That's the last straw. I lunge for his throat. Hopefully I can wrap my hands around his neck and wring it out.

Chapter 7

Phantom's green eyes lightly glow in the dark like mine sometimes do. I tremble, but conceal it since the last thing I need is for him to know what his secret lair does to me. It makes me extremely nervous, being who knows where and alone with the most dangerous man on the planet. My mind was sending off alarm signals which makes my muscles tense up and on high alert. If Phantom crossed one toe over the line, then I'd whack him so hard that hopefully I'd knock him out.

He chuckles lightly, and runs a hand through my long blonde hair, "I like you on my bed," he lightly puts a hand on my shoulder. " Relax."

But his comment doesn't necessarily help me to relax. In fact, it definitely did the exact opposite, making my skin tingle in an alarming way. He has to know what he is doing to me. That must be why he's acting this way, I reason.

"You have to answer my questions, you know," I squeak out like a mouse.

I hear the light thud as Phantom's boots finally touch the floor. He's always hovering slightly about the ground, enough that sometimes I do not realize that he is hovering. I chastise myself for missing that piece of information. He bows his head down to mine so I can feel the light pressure of his minty breath and whispers, "I don't think you'd want to know, Chaos. Maybe I think that it would be a burden on you if I tell you everything I know. What if you already had enough worries on your little mind that I believe telling you exactly what kind of dangers we'll have to face or avoid," he pauses to stress the last part for a brief moment before continuing, "you'll then ruin my carefully set up, but oh-so fragile plan I have brewed. Can't have that now can we?" I could feel his eyebrow lift up at me suggestively.

I shake my head, "But what can you tell me? Why is Anigirl in so much danger? How am I supposed to protect her when I don't know what I'm up against! You know just as well as I do that some villains are out there who can squash my life like a bug!"

Phantom smiles and I could hear the gears in his brain turning to imagine me getting squashed by his chunky yet sleek boots. "That is why I personally have a long hit-list. You, my dear, have lots of haters... including Maine Jerrs. If Maine ever targeted me, I'd go into permanent hiding- something you haven't done."

I blink as Phantom mentions my mother's name. She is locked up nice and tight in a padded room with a visit from a psychologist every other hour.

"Ugh, Maine doesn't matter, she's in the super prison and is never getting out. It's the other villains that I'm worried about," I huff angrily.

"No, Maine does matter. She matters more than you think. In fact, all of the Jerrs have bigger roles than you might think," Phantom sighs, lying down on the bed with his arms behind his head. I feel the bed shift and decide to sit across the bed on a black leather sofa. Even in the dark, I know all the pieces of furniture. This isn't my first rodeo in Phantom's lair.

I hear him groan out to me, but choose to ignore it. He can complain all he wants that I refuse to 'snuggle' with him.

"How that heck do all the Jerrs matter?" I ask, voice super sharp. I am not messing around. How do my parents, and I matter in his big scheme?

"Not all. Just two. Maine and whatever demon she's keeping inside of her. You know, Kelsey Jerrs lives with Anigirl. They're BFFs, and she's the best candidate to be you. She shows absolutely no signs of having any powers, but we both know that it's impossible for her not to have any gifts. Chaos, I have to know, are you Kelsey Jerrs?" he asks seriously.

I shake my head, not that Phantom could notice that in the dark unless he uses his night vision, which I'm not sure he is, "Absolutely not!"

"Liar," Phantom says lazily.

"No, I'm really not. I swear I'm not Kelsey Jerrs," I try to cover.

Suddenly, Phantom is straddling my lap, his face very close to mine. Our noses brush and he laughs evilly. He's heavy in my lap, but Phantom doesn't care about my discomfort.

"Ugh, get away!" I growl, trying to shove him off.

"I'm missing your witty retorts. Have I figured it out? Chaos is," he lowers his voice dangerously in my ear, "Kelsey? It makes sense because you've said that you're name isn't even close to your superhero name.

"Do you really want to know?" I squeak after a long pause of silence. Phantom shrugs his deliciously broad shoulders in a reply.

"I am not Kelsey Jerrs," I deadpan, looking right into those green eyes that mirror mine.

"You're lying, but I'll play your little game. Besides, when Rush asks me, I don't have to lie. I'm not a liar... unlike somebody in this room," he scoffs indignantly at me.

My hands clench into tight fists. Phantom is a complete liar! What is his deal?

"Whaaat? No witty remark? Has my perfection and beauty stunned Chaos into absolute silence? I can live with you shutting up. In fact, I've been waiting since the first time we fought for you to shut that peep hole of yours," Phantom laughs, and I wince since the laugh is nothing but harsh.

"Suck on a Ring Pop, Phantom!" I hiss, eyes narrowing to small slits.

He opens his mouth the reply, pauses, then closes it. "You actually told me what to suck. Kudos to you!" he says after a few moments of eyeing my smug smile.

"I've learned from the best," I reply curtly. Once I told Phantom to 'suck it' and his reply was 'okay, then come here'. Remembering that embarrassing situation, I shudder.

He purrs. Yes, actual purring came out of those lips. A lot of his fan girls think that's the sexiest sound that has ever protruded out of a man's mouth, but to me... the noise is infuriating. "I can teach you a lot more, if you'd let me. Want to hear my syllabus I have for when you finally accept my offer?"

I try to reply, but cannot since he begins to twirl some of my hair around his finger. He sighs, and my face is blasted with a minty scent from his toothpaste. I put some more distance between our faces.

"First, I'm going to teach you how to actually hurt someone, and the best ways to inflict pain. Second, I'm going to make you work out so hard that you'll be putty in my hands at night, but I wouldn't take advantage of you yet because you'll be in so much pain that you'll hate my very existence- no matter how hard that is for you to do now. Third, I'm going to put you up against my friends, and see if you can come out on top. By this point you might like me enough so I use you then, but I'm guessing that part will come on the fourth part. The fourth part is that I'll tell you my plan and we will execute it perfectly and without any questions. Do you still want to decline my offer?" he asks, a tiny bit of hope at the last sentence.

"Heck no! I'd rather sleep in a vat of lava than have you 'take advantage' of me!" I shake my head, and push him off of my lap.

"Surpass is going to get Maine out of her prison cell thingy, and then you'll come crying to me. But don't worry my little superhero Chaos, my arms will be wide open to receive you."

I stare at him, imagining beating the smirk off of his face. I've done it before- hit him so hard that he lost consciousness. The police captured him while he was out, too. Needless to say Anna and I went out to Olive Garden to celebrate that night. I know that Phantom's fingerprints are all burned off, and that the identification system couldn't find a match on him from the reports. Of course, once Phantom awoke, he just walked through the bars and murdered all the cops at the station (which were only a few since Hyptonic, another villain, was almost ending the world and the superhero who's in charge of that area was a no show) and then he wiped all reports and anything the police might have come by while he was inside the cell.

Yeah, that night at four in the morning Phantom hunted my rear down and gave me a nice reprimand. And by a nice reprimand I mean he kicked my butt out to Washington, drove his little black Range Rover to where I was, then kicked my behind so excruciatingly hard I was screaming all the way to Pennsylvania.

That must be the reason why I'm not one of the top ten superheroes...

"Right," I snort.

He cups my face with his hands, "I'll protect you from your mother," he says seriously.

"You're a villain. Villain 101 must have told you that you should not care for the hero. I suppose you didn't pay attention?" I shoot back.

"There's the wit I was longing for. Welcome back, Chaos." he winks before responding, "Well I got the Being a Villain for Dummies book, but as you know I don't read books. Ever."

I roll my eyes, "Then why do you have a bookshelf across the room?"

"Just because I have them does not mean I read them," he states in a sing-song voice.

"Okay, so when Maine gets out with the help of Surpass- do you know his identity?" I pause for a moment, and Phantom doesn't interrupt me as I instantly change tracks. "Holy crap..." I gasp in horror. My body is so stiff underneath Phantom's butt that I'm sure it must be uncomfortable for him to continue to sit on my lap.

"Phantom..." I try to say what is on my mind, but my breathing becomes shallow as I realize the probability that what I thought of could be right.

He slides off of my lap, and his hands drift down to my shoulders, "Chaos, don't have a panic attack. Do not panic."

I tried to even out my breathing. My hands clenched my skirt as I focused. Yeah, I so don't want a panic attack right now. That would be so embarrassing, I chant to myself in my head.

When Phantom sees that I'm somewhat okay he asks the question, "What have you conjured up that I have not figure out?"

I inhale a shaky breath, "W-what if whoever Surpass's identity is... is working as... as one of Maine's therapists?"

There is not a single noise as Phantom thinks of what I have just said. One could hear a pin drop, or cut the tension with a knife if they were in the room.

He says a reaaaally bad word.

Chapter 8

I tense up, and our eyes lock. Mine are wide with fear, because if Surpass has been keeping in touch with my mother, then that would mean...

Kelsey Jerrs was never safe. My life isn't safe. Anna's family is in danger.

I repeat the synonym for crap that Phantom used. A side of his mouth twitches up for less that a nanosecond. Our minds whirl at a million miles an hour and they cannot slow down as we figure out all the possible reasons and all the possible plans that Maine could brew up with Surpass. There are too many. My breaths come in short gasps as the variables overload my brain.

Phantom's eyes soften as they keep gazing back at me. I look at the ground between my knees as I pant.

How long have they been planning? How intricate is the scheme? How terrified should I be right now? When will the plan become actions rather than words? When? Where? Why? How?

Phantom suddenly takes my chin in his hand and tilts it up. My lips part as I struggle for oxygen, my body begins to shake. Those unforgiving green eyes take me in, and suddenly my body presses against his. My ear is to his chest and I can hear his steady heartbeat.

Is this a panic attack? I've only read about them. One other time, Phantom gave me a panic attack. He kissed me, and I was fine. I didn't want him to kiss me again! I had to get myself under control. He's the villain, not my hero!

I try to keep my undeady breathing untraceable from his notice-if Phantom already didn't notice. But I know he has noticed already, but he just wants to see how everything plays out before he stepped in during the last possible second.

We are both waiting for that last second. I didn't want it to come, and Phantom was patiently waiting for it, the corners of his mouth twitching up.

"Chaos? Are you okay?" he asks, knowing full well what is happening because it's happened before. "Don't tell me... you're having a panic attack?Information overload, you're numerical brain can't handle too many 'what ifs' so it is freaking out. We've been on this road before, so I have just the remedy..." Phantom tilts his face towards mine extremely slowly. Taking his time.

Those eyes pierce mine and I stop breathing as his breath fans across my lips. I can taste the mint, how does he always have minty breath? He holds the position, and then an evil laugh escapes his lips.

"Mwah," he kisses my forehead and I freeze with shock.

"All better. Doctor Phantom fixed you all up. Know you can breathe, and I didn't have to kiss you- thank the heavens," he puts his gloved hands together like a prayer, and looks up the ceiling.

"What?" I ask, my brain unable to keep up.

He gives me an annoyed look, "Did you hear 'make out session' in my grand plan before? Because that happens after you accept my glorious offer of training. And of course, after you stop hurting so bad that you sleep right after training... Semantics," Phantom sticks his tongue out at me.

"What are the odds that Maine is already at Anigirl's house?" I cut in.

Phantom smirks at me, "Oh, about ninety percent. The real question is, will Kelsey Jerrs be there and will Maine have killed her or tied her up? I hope if the kid did die, that her brains will be blown out. I love a good shotgun bullet to the head, it turns me on better than you could if you attempted to dirty talk me."

"Sadistic," I note.

"Just how you like," he fires back. I bite my lip.

"I wouldn't know," I retort after a moment.

"Yes, because you're a virgin, and I still hate that fact. Haven't I taught you any flirting skills?" he keeps ranting.

That wasn't where I want to go with the conversation, "I meant I wouldn't know the odds of Maine shooting Kelsey or not."

"Sure you did. Admit it, you're mind has been in the gutter since I brought you back to a room with a bed in it. We both want it, so it's okay to confess. I won't tell anyone," he smiles a fake smile that is sickly sweet it makes me sick.

"No? That's okay, you're face is an open book. Well, I suppose we both will have to see if Maine is at the Henderson's or not. However, there is no way Phantom is going to drive by that house. I'll be darned if Maine sees Phantom. She'll mar my perfect face!" he adds a theatrical gasp at the end, and caresses the side of his own face in an extremely creepy way.

"Can't have that, can you?" I roll my eyes sarcastically.

He sits on my lap again, and I am beginning to think that he likes having me between his legs. He straddles my waist and those arms wrap abound my shoulders.

"You like to be on top, don't you?" I ask.

Phantom bursts out in laughter, "As a matter of fact, yes. But it's not about control, if you're wondering- and I'm positive you are wondering. You'll find out why lat-er," he emphasizes the last word more than usual and a hand runs down the back of my bicep. The cold leather of his gloves make me shiver.

He practically purrs.

"Okaaay! Well, I must be going to check out the world. You know, there are other villains out there besides you I have to worry about," I say trying to get up. It's impossible and by the way Phantom's eyes lower to slits I'm sure that he doesn't want me to leave.

He holds my waist down to the chair, "Maine will kill you, Chaos. You cannot afford to face her! With my training you might stand a chance. Heck, you can't even defeat me! What are you supposed to do once Kelsey's mother or even Surpress himself shows up?" he runs his fingers through my hair, effectively musing it up, "Don't make me lose you too," he whispers so quietly. Pain flashes in those eyes for a moment, and I realize that I hardly know Phantom.

"You won't," I say.

He laughs humorlessly, "I could tie you to this chair. I could knock you unconscious right now to keep you from going back. I'm sadistic, remember? You're my personal toy to maul."

I gasp at the sting of his words, and one of his fingers glide down my spine. He doesn't truly mean that. He couldn't.

"My word, it's not like I'm going to die! How boring would that be? Get killed fighting Maine- a woman who's possessed by a blood thirsty demon thing that has made a cozy Motel 6 out of her body. Lame ending, for sure," I shove his shoulder to try to get him off of me.

Phantom rummages in one of the pouches in his belt, and pulls out a thin needle full of clear liquid.

"Shoot! Get that away from me!" I cry out. Phantom knows how much I hate needles. He looks from the needle to me, and then back to the needle again. "Phantom I'm serious! Get. That. Away!"

With one move, he captures my arm, and rests it against the armrest of the chair. Our eyes lock in a silent challenge.

"Don't," I whisper, breaking the eye contact because A- his eyes are freaky green, and B- the needle was getting dangerously close to my arm.

"I don't want to lose you. I've never wanted to kill you. The first time we met, I knew that I would end up having feelings for you. I mean, how can a boy not like you- the slim-waisted, platinum blonde model with legs that stretch on and on for miles and a drop dead gorgeous smile? You've made me want to be good, but that's something I can never be. I hate rules too much, and I have too many enemies," Phantom states. His forehead drops to my chest and I know that the position is not in any way comfortable.

In any case, Phantom just stated that he has feelings for me. I felt a jolt of excitement run through me at the thought. 'Slim-waisted', 'model', and 'drop dead gorgeous' just came out of his mouth to describe not Anigirl, not some movie star, but me.

It is like the Fourth of July as my brain exploded in a million different colors. And then I feel the slight prick of a needle entering my vein.

"YOU BLOODY ANIMAL!" I shriek in a British accent for some reason. It is a good thing one of his arms are holding my arm down, and his thighs lock my waist to the chair, otherwise I would have flung him through the wall, new tailored suit or not.

Phantom tilts his head to the side, "Does that count as you saying a bad word even though we're Americans? You did say it in a British accent, young lady."

Oh yeah, I thought, He keeps a tally of everytime I say a bad word in his presence.

Then there was absolute darkness as whatever was in the needle runs it course through my blood.

Chapter 9

When I wake up, my head feels like a brick and my face is nestled into the front lawn of Anna's home. I jerk up and think about all the ants that could be on my face. I don't particularly like grass, and if it's freshly mowed I hate it even more. This lawn was always freshly cut. Mr. Henderson is very peculiar about it being cut and inch tall.

I get up and run my gloved hand across the side of my mouth. My cheeks redden as I realize that I totally drooled and I take a big gulp, looking around. Nobody has seen me. Me? I reach up to the short platinum blonde. Yeah, I am Chaos still, I breathe a sigh of relief. What would I have done if I am Kelsey? Phantom is nowhere I can sense him, and I walk up to the front door.

Oh, Mother please don't be here! I think as I walk up to the front door. When I reach it I realize that maybe coming from the front door isn't the best idea if Maine was in there or not. I turn on the heel of my chunky combat boots and walk past the garage towards the back gate. With extreme caution

I unlatch the gat and swing the gate wide enough so that it wouldn't creak open.

If Maine wasn't here and Anna or her parents saw me, I'd have lots is explaining to do. It was so strange for someone to enter the house through the back door. I didn't want to come off as peculiar and make Anna wonder. When she wants to know something then there is no way for her not to know it. That is why I need to be careful as I look for any tell-tale signs of my mother's pleasant visit discreetly as possible.

The back door requires a key but my bedroom window would be easier to slip through than risk getting caught by a chef or Anna. I peer over the window well before stepping onto the first rung of the small ladder that acts like a fire escape. I climb down carefully and face the window. I feel the pleasant vibration as my body turns intangible as I walk through the window panes.

Once in my room I look around for any animal that Rush could be before slipping out of my Chaos clothes and into a 'Future Harvard/Stanford/Yale Student' on the front in black box letters. Honestly, I have no will to go to any of those colleges- not that my grades are good enough any who- but Anna got the shirt for me and so I wear it to please her good will. The shirt looks the best when paired with my black sweatpants that Mrs. Henderson absolutely hates me to wear. I pull them on anyways, since the thought of dressing up for my mother is appalling.

I quietly pull out a lock picking kit from under the sofa cushions. I hide most of my Chaos tools in between the couch cushions and underneath the couch and the bed.

Sometimes, I put the items-like a small pistol I got from my apartment when Mom was arrested and a few... other things I shouldn't have- in a black box that has stuffed animals on top in my closet. I don't have many items that are personal to me but that pistol is one of my treasures. I believe Mom may have used it to kill Dad if he was dead. I have nothing to know about my father but I do know that Mom loved that pistol very much. And so I took it before the cops could commandeer it.

Knowing that I have that pistol, even if Mom doesn't know I have it, made me feel safer. It is the security that one has when having leverage over another, and that is a relief.

I pocket the lock picking kit and step out into the hall. I pause and debate if I should change or not. If Phantom hasn't left me then I'd be able to feel his powers, which I do not. Maybe Phantom is expecting Kelsey to be here, maybe not. But Kelsey isn't here so I wonder what Phantom would do if he knew that. He'd probably go search for her. The first stop would be wherever Anna is.

I walk to Anna's door to her room. She's not in it, but her bed is a huge mess of clothes, hair accessories, papers, notecards, and pens. I scrunch my nose up at the sight. My room is always cleaner than hers except when Phantom keeps me so busy during the week.

Mother, what are you planning?

I silently shut the door and walk towards the stairs. I creep up them cautiously. Nobody seems to be in the mansion. How strange.

When reaching the main floor I decide to play it safe and turn invisible. There's less to worry about when nobody can see you. I tread carefully in my boots, which is an art Phantom told me is possible in the beginning of my superhero career. Sound is my worst enemy at the moment and so I take my time scouring each office, room and the kitchen. I poke my head through closed doors so that I don't have to open them and scan the empty rooms that are hardly ever used in the first place. There is nothing so I tread up to the second floor.

Anna's school papers litter the coffee table in the hall to the master bedroom. I halt to peek at them. One paper has today's date on it so I know she's been here after school. Upon furthering my attempt of investigating, I realize that there is not hidden message or code that Anna left behind. That can be a good or a bad sign, but I hope for the best because she doesn't know anything.

Not knowing is dangerous. The thought makes me worry about Anna. I don't put it past Maine to take her as a means to get whatever she wants. Maybe Phantom is wrong and she wants Anna like the rest of the villains want Anigirl. Maine could easily have figured out that Anigirl is Anna. As easily as Phantom did.

I swallow hard at the thought and push it out of my head. I need to know what the villains are planning and how Maine's plan fit in with it all.

What's your angle, Mom?

I enter the master suite by going through the door. Phantom lies in the center of the huge bed and I bite my lip to keep from screaming in shock. His legs are crossed, the buttons of his suit jacket are open revealing a dark gray shirt, and those green eyes are aimed at me.

"About time. Man, Chaos, I was beginning to worry that maybe Maine was in this house and she got you. How lame," he pokes his tongue out at me.

How did I not sense him? Well, he wasn't using his powers if that helps. I make myself known with a long sigh, "You dumped me in the front freakin' yard."

He laughed, "You were drooling on my suit. Again."

I shrug my shoulders, "If you don't like me drooling all over you, then don't knock me out."

He smirks, "Oh I wouldn't mind if you drooled all over me, because that will happen... eventually and we'll both enjoy it immensely."

I make a fake gagging noise that is not attractive at all, "So you keep alluding to."

"It will happen eventually. After you agree for me to train you. How scared were you as you searched the Henderson's home for your mother?"

I clench my fists at my sides, "Maine is not my mother. I am not Kelsey. I wasn't the least bit afraid but I will admit that I was nervous. Being nervous about something and earning something are two extremely different emotions, Phantom. Not that you would know of course, seeing how you don't have any feelings whatsoever."

He groans, but a smile plays on his lips, "Low blow using the feeling card."

"Get out of here Phantom. We both don't belong in the Henderson's estate."

With that I saunter towards the balcony doors, open them and jump down to the grass. There's a way to survive a jump like that, and it's called making your bones intangible for only a millisecond as the impact spears through the body. An extremely hard trick that I came up with myself. Phantom just floats down after me.

Note to self: straighten out bed spread of Anna's parent's room.

"I can teach you how to hover," he states proudly.

"Like I'd ever agree to your tutor services," I shoot back.

"Sometimes I wish that you'd fight with Maine and get common sense knocked into you. Don't worry Chaos, I have broad shoulders for you to come cry on once you get whacked in the face with a substantially large dose of a drug I like to call reality."

I grind my teeth together, "Like I'd come crying to you!"

He shrugs those broad shoulders at me, "Only time will tell."

Then he poofs into thin air and I know he is gone. For a moment I stand there and wonder how he could do that. It's a trick that Phantom shows no interest to share with me. I suppose it is for good reason. If I knew how to poof away then if he tries to lock me up or kidnap me then I'd just vanish. He does that to me when he doesn't like the way I catch him in a headlock, or there's nothing sexual about the way I tie him up. Phantom is quite the diva.

With a sigh I turn back to the house and once again make my way to the backyard and down the window well to my room. I change into gray shorts that reach to my fingertips and a Mickey Mouse T-shirt. I run my fingers through my now long black hair and know that I am now Kelsey.

I open the door and once again step out. Nobody is in the house and I sigh. Being alone really sucks lollipops for me. I used to always be alone while Maine was out robbing or killing people. Being alone with only thought to accompany one's self isn't fun.

I sit down on the couch and flick on the T.V. screen to a cartoon. There are DVD cases to the left of the T.V. screen that have seasons of shows on the disk. I think about popping in the fourth season of White Collar or the second season of the original Teen Titans- Anna's favorite kid show when she was younger, but settle on Kelly & Michael reruns instead. The noise drowns out my thoughts as I just mindlessly stare at the screen, lounging on the couch and taking up most of the room. It doesn't matter, I reason, because it isn't like Anna is here to share the couch with anyways.

I debate whether or not to do Pre-Calc homework but decide against it. I miss the sound of the front door opening but then I hear Anna yell, "I'm home peeps!"

And the worry that Maine could have my best friend disappears. So if she isn't after Anna, then what does Maine want?

Chapter 10

When school rolls back around I am not become a happy camper. Mainly I am upset over Anna for being so careless. First, this morning when I woke up and pulled myself out of my room to the sofa to sleep ten minutes more, those ten minutes ended up being an hour because Anna-darn her to the deepest pit it Hades- decided to leave early with her two guy friends, Ryan and Luis so they can 'study' for the major test they had in Algebra. Studying is okay in my book, but she didn't tell me beforehand so when I woke up and freaked out that she didn't wake me up I searched for her to find that Mrs. Henderson knew that Anna was 'studying' with her guy friends, and then Mrs. Henderson stated that school started ten minutes ago and I had a mother freak out session in the kitchen, with a young, dark haired cook witnessing the whole thing.

"She should tell me these things! Anna is so dead when I get my hands on her-" I began but Mrs. Henderson saved my life by glancing at the young male cook and then back to me.

I promptly shut my pie hole and grabbed an apple to serve as breakfast.

I didn't leave the kitchen fast enough to hear Anna's mom release a long sigh, "Finally she eats something healthy for breakfast! I've been trying to get Kelsey off sugar cereal for years!"

I laughed really loud in the doorframe. Phantom's words registering in my head. He likes my curves, so I have nothing to fret about.

"An apple hardly is breakfast," the boy replied.

"I know, but it's a start."

I ran down the stairs to get ready and arrived at school forty-five minutes late. It was too late for me to go to first hour and the middle of second, so I interrupted the class to get to my seat, half eaten apple in hand. That is fine except that on my way to. My desk, Tera Sullhem tripped me so I fell in the middle of the aisle of desks. I had to twist so I didn't land on the apple in my hand and fell on my side.

The fake linoleum floor did nothing to cushion the brunt of the impact on my arm. Pain spread like wildfire and I cried out making Tera laugh evilly.

Tera and I have a past full of violence on my part. I punched her into the hallway lockers when she made Anna cry Sophomore year. Of course I got suspended, and it was the blip on my record I told Phantom about, but it was worth it.

Oh man, was suspension worth it.

She didn't get suspended but spend a few days in the hospital because I gave her a concussion. Her parents were royally pissed at me, but they didn't press charges or anything- which I was extremely lucky because the Sullhems sued about everything they thought wrong with the world.

Mrs. Henderson chastised me a bit but I didn't get into trouble for sticking up for her daughter. She only lectured how I should have gone to a teacher or taken the issue up with the front office. Mr. Henderson bought me a beat up minivan that I named Jorge in celebration even though I wasn't yet sixteen. Jorge is parked outside of the huge garage because it really is a piece of poop car. I didn't need to use it much, so I took out the third row of seats and stocked it with Chaos stuff in case of emergency. I am the only one who has the keys to that car, so the fear that some houseworker would find the cases of first aid kits, Gothic outfits, a few weapons hidden under the seats with extra ammunition, and two sleeping bags that fit two people in one just in case Phantom or Rush needed solace.

Not that that would ever happen.

I stand up and sit in my seat. My cheeks warm with extra blood and I know my round face resembles a tomato.

"Watch where you're going, Jerrs!" Tera laughs.

I flip her off without the teacher seeing.

"Oooh," Tera rolls her eyes like it wasn't a big deal. I scoff and turn towards the teacher who is asking if I am alright or not.

"I'm okay," I say sweetly just for Terra's benefit. My arm stings, so I rub it a bit, thinking that the pain will disappear. The pain still throbs but I ignore it.

My partner completely ignores me and I inspect my arm. No visible damage that I can see but it hurts very badly. My first thought is that I might have broken it, but I assume that if I did break it, then there would be more pain and I would definitely know that my arm is broken.

Can't be that, I chant in my head. If for some reason I needed a cast, then Chaos would have a cast too, and that would be obvious to everyone that I am Chaos. That cannot happen.

The bell rings and I grab my bag and sling it over my shoulder. Pre-Calc is next and I smile at the thought. Rather than go right away to class, I swing by where Anna is walking to her class and intercept her.

"Anna!" I call to get her attention. She turn towards me and rushed to grab both of my arms.

"Kelsey! Mom texted me and to me that you were late to school! I am so sorry! I knew I shouldn't have gone but there was this huge test and I was going to fail it until the boys offered to study. I think I did so much bett- what's wrong?" she asks, finally noticing my grimace of pain as the hold on my arm resembles a vice.

I shrug, "Terra tripped me in second period and I landed on my arm. It hurts so much, but it can't be broken so I don't know what's wrong with it."

Anna's brown eyes widen at me, "What if it is broken? What is," she lowers her voice in the middle of hundreds of people, "Chaos going to do if you get a cast?"

I gesture that I have no clue what would happen as the warning bell rings and we both stiffen, being far away from our classes.

"I gotta go. If your arm keeps bothering you then call Mom to take you to the hospital," Anna instructs before bouncing off. I watch as her two long braids bounce off her back to fly into the air, and I shake my head before hustling to my own class.

By lunch, my arm is slightly blue, which I figure isn't a good thing. I call Mrs. Henderson but she doesn't answer. Anna nods at me from across the table so I leave a voicemail saying that I fell and landed on my arm and that now it is kind of blue looking. She should get the hint that it's serious.

"Oh. My. Gosh! You kissed Noah Cardinale?" A voice screeches through the cafeteria. Nobody had to look up to know that it is a girl with the last name Fern, who always goes by her last name for some reason. This girl is Tessa's rumor machine, so Tessa keeps her among the tight circle she thinks are friends.

The cafeteria goes silent so it is easy to hear Tessa stage whisper, "Sh! It's a secret!"

Everyone sees through the act, returning to their conversations. My phone beeps with Twitter notifications and I groan. Let the talk begin.

Anna turns to me, "Isn't your English teacher dating a Cardinale?"

I nod my head and take time to smooth out my uniform skirt, "Miss Benson is dating Hayden- the oldest one."

She takes a bite of her sandwich and chews on it for a bit before swallowing. "You know, I thought the Cardinale boys all had enough brains not to date someone like Tessa. All she wants is his body, the fame, expensive dates, and the mind blowing-"

I cut her off, "I really don't care what she wants out of Noah. In fact, I couldn't care less then I already do, which by the way is nothing because I do not give a rat's butt about it."

"A rat's butt?" Anna questions, looking at me like I am some rare specimen of goo she is studying.

I nod as my phone rings and the ID shows that it is Mrs. Henderson so I answer it.

"In coming to school right now to take you to the doctor. Don't go to your next class!" she pants like she ran a marathon. Mrs. Henderson probably did, so I smile at the thought.

"Okay, will do," I say looking down at my arm. Instead of blue, it's a dark purple and Anna gulps loud enough for me to hear.

"Whatever you do, do not panic about your arm," Mrs. Henderson orders.

"Okay, okay. Tell me where to meet you?" I release a loud sigh and the back of my neck bristles. Phantom is here. My eyes immediately scan the room, but I know he's probably sitting in the empty chair next to Anna, dress shoes up on the plastic tabletop.

I stand up, stuffing my halfway eaten lunch back into the brown paper bag and putting it in my backpack.

"My word! Your arm looks purple!" Anna gasps.

"I'm hoping it's just a nasty bruise and that it isn't broken," I reply.

"I think it's broken- if not fractured," she huffs.

I smirk and turn around. Tessa is right there, standing next to one did the baseball boys, her long noodle arms around his waist, her cheek pressed against his back.

"I thought you kissed Noah Cardinale? With the whole show and all, I actually might have believed it. Don't tell me you're cheating on him with a baseball player!" I gasp at Tessa.

She sneers at me, which makes her face look very unattractive, well, the half of it that wasn't plastered to the baseball player's back anyway.

"Go die Jerrs!" she cackles.

I roll my eyes and put a hand on my hip, "You know, my mom tried to kill me multiple times but it didn't work. I'd think of something a bit more creative than that when your trying to rip out my soul to feed your own ego."

She grits her teeth and Anna stifles a laugh. I never really tell anything about what my mom did to me while she was being possessed by a demon. Anna and her parents don't even know the whole story.

I pat her head of blonde hair with my good arm, "Aw, don't worry Tessa. If you keep frowning like that then you'll get nasty wrinkles. Wouldn't want that now would we?"

She opens he mouth to retort hit no sound comes out. I win this round.

"Toodles!" I wave goodbye to Tessa and Anna as I exit the cafeteria, trying not to shiver with Phantom's presence of him using his abilities.

He probably just witnessed that whole ordeal, I realize. I groan and shake my head of black hair, it was a show to be seen, that is for sure.

I smile to myself and wait as Mrs. Henderson comes to pick me up.

Hopefully my arm isn't broken.

Chapter 11

The words reverberate throughout my skull. Words of a news reporter with breaking news that almost broke me.

"Through the first week of this month, occurrences of murder have been reported. No eyewitnesses were at the scenes on both the Werrither family homicide and the Wothing home armed robbery earlier this month. At first Sheriff Hill insisted that these occurrences were two very separate ordeals, however; just this last night, surveillance cameras on the Wurdson home shows a women figure in a tightly drawn black cape breaking through on the the back windows. Nothing so far has been reported missing or stolen, and no one in the Wurdson home was killed.

"This woman could be Maine Jerrs who escaped her padded cell near the end of last month. She is very dangerous to herself and others. Heroes from all over the USA are looking out for her. Maine Jerrs is a women who is believed to be possessed by a demon who loves to kill. When she was convicted, the list includes attempted and successful murder, homicide, robbery, aiding villains, and a hundred attempts of fraud..."

Maine is after the Ws right now and then who will she target once every last name beginning with a W is checked off the list?

I didn't have a doubt that Mom was behind the three robberies. I know her well enough to play her stupid games. This game was tricky, but I had played it before without even Phantom's help and won. If needs be, I can play it again.

Rule One to play my Mother's sick and sadistic game: meet at the starting point.

Where would that point be? The one place we both know cops will search first and never return to again, the place where Mom feels the most comfortable, and I feel the most pain. The apartment where I used to live before rooming up with Anna and the Hendersons.

The apartment is way downtown. Some call this place the Dumps because there were no hones, just run down apartment complexes and fancy business buildings and evil factories that puffed crap into the air, giving the Dumps a smokey black sky in place of the light blue, and a really rancid smell. Growing up, I lived here and was completely happy here. Of course, I didn't know that the corner of my apartment building was nicknamed Rape Corner, and I didn't understand why so many apartments had red lights on their front porches in place or normal lights.

The Dumps is the city's best kept secret. Nobody ever comes down here to visit, and that is exactly the way the residents want it to be. The rich in one side of the city, the Dumps on the other, with this strange and awkward mix in the middle.

Of course I didn't drive to the Dumps, but I did drive to the center of town and parked Jorge in the mall parking lot even though technically I don't have my license. The mall is neutral ground that everyone can mix and mingle together. Behind the stores, people sell drugs, bodies, and over-the-counter medication but at least the cops aren't afraid to do a routine check behind the mall every half hour at different parts of that half hour.

Cops hardly ever venture into the Dumps, unless they are from the Dumps.

I cut through the mall instead of walking around the outside to get to my location. People bustle to and fro and I am careful not to bump into them. I have nothing on me, not even a few dollars and definitely not a purse. That's an unspoken rule in the Dumps, those who have purses won't have them for very long.

I am close to the end of the mall, where there are few people, when a black glove grasps my shoulder and spins me around.

"And just where do you think you are going?" Phantom purrs into my ear.

"My mother is out there!" I exclaim, ripping my shoulder from his tight grip.

"Are you meeting her?" he asks like it would be the worst idea ever to meet her.

"If she is where I know she would be, then yes."

Phantom chuckles but there is nothing humorous about his laugh. I grind my teeth together and look him in the eyes, "Go screw yourself, Phantom!"

"Sassy..." he pokes his tongue out at my direction but I spin on my heel and continue to walk.

"It takes two to tango, Kelsey Jerrs!" he retorts. "Plus, I would personally count that use of screw as a naughty, naughty word. I name my price for you to tell my if you're Chaos. I know you are, but I want to hear those words come out of your mouth."

I groan and continue walking. He doesn't stop me but begins to walk with me instead.

"You walk like Chaos does, the slight swing of your hips. FYI I think you could run the catwalk with that swing it is so subtly sexy. I also love the black Goth vibe you're working, it's definitely hot. You look almost unattainable and intense but I can break those defenses," he rambles.

I glare at him, "Shut up! I am N-O-T Chaos! I don't even know what you're doing here. Leave me alone."

"Aw, you are smokin' when you're pissed. I am dishing out compliments to you like they're candy and you won't eat a single piece," Phantom frowns.

"Maybe because I know villains enough to know that everything they do comes with a price or they're trying to obtain something of mine. I believe that you want to distract me from going to my Mother's home. News flash: it's my home too. I may live with the Hendersons but I belong in the Dumps."

"People belong where they want to belong. I think you can bloom in rich society. The Dumps will smother you," he pokes my cheek with a gloved index finger.

I stop in my tracks. He stops and I grind my heel into the toes of his nice dress shoes, "Stop. Acting. Like. You. Know. Me!"

"But I do know you, Chaos. I would venture to say that I know your secrets better than Anna," he smirks as I stop grinding my heel into his shoes and find that there isn't even a mark on the leather exterior that's left.

"I'm not frigging Chaos! You don't know me! Stop doing this to me Phantom! Please!"

His face softens, and his arms wrap around my waist, "You're so nervous your body is ice and your hands are shaking violently. Let me protect you, Kelsey."

"You are the villain who's been ruining my life with whatever stunt you decide to pull on nights I always have tests. Remember when you knocked me unconscious on top of the Mayor's building and left me there? That wasn't protecting me!" I yell.

Those green eyes widen and mine do too. I begin to run out the back of the mall and I keep running, even though Phantom is close behind me.

He doesn't know where I am going. If I turn invisible he'd lose me.

I ponder that thought as my feet cross the literal line into the place I came from.

No going back now, I think eerily to myself. My pace doesn't slow as I cross the line and my senses fill with the disgusting scent of the factories. I risk to glacé behind my to see Phantom also crossing the line. He's not a bit nervous, something tells me that Phantom had been here before. Chaos never met him in the Dumps before.

I veer into a vapor shop that I know has a back exit easily accessible to customers. My black bear up ankle boots pound into the tile floor as the sweet smell of vapors reach my nose, mixing with the awful factory smell.

Phantom reaches out and grabs my arm before I can reach the door and turn invisible, "I know what you're planning, Kelsey. Don't do it."

I yank my arm out of his grip, but he captures my other arm even harder. I know that this vice like grip I cannot get out of no matter how hard I try.

He leads me to the back door, the people at the hookahs and behind the counters are too stoned to intervene. We exit and Phantom presses my body against the wall, "What the eff are you thinking?" he swears.

"I count that as a naughty, naughty word," I gasp as his forearm presses against my collarbone so I cannot escape.

"I have every right to swear! You're going to get yourself effing killed!" he yells.

"That's two," I gasp, needing oxygen.

"Shall I bend you over my thighs and spank your butt like a five-year-old?" Phantom threatens darkly.

I gulp realizing that he is majorly upset- and that's putting it lightly. "You owe me two requests so here they are: first, don't follow me and second-"

Smack!

I inhale so sharply that I choke on air. My rear end stings and I wonder how the crap he did that while I'm being shoved against the wall.

"That's inappropriate!" I scream. My cheeks deepen in color.

"You're being stupid! If you join Maine's stupid little game she set up, then you'll die."

"You don't know that. How do you know when you don't have a clue what she's planning? FYI, I'm pretty sure I can handle my own mother. I've played her games before- Don't spank me again! I swear to everything-!" I cut myself off as realization ignites in my eyes.

"I've talked to her, Kelsey."

I swallow hard and remain silent.

"I know what she's planning. I know how to get that demon out of her. I know things that I want to teach you but you won't freaking let me. Don't go to your mother. Not yet at least. People will die, but you can avenge their deaths. Let me help you and you can help me," Phantom's eyes pierce mine and I can't look away. Those eyes plead with mine silently until I release a deep sigh.

"Fine. Teach me what you know so I can save my mom."

Phantom smiles at me, and our bodies turn intangible and we descend below the surface. His arms tightly embrace me and I remind myself to breathe even though we are under feet of dirt. My fingers clutch the back of his white shirt and I hide my face in his chest.

"We are saving my mom, not killing her, right?" I ask.

"Of course," Phantom replies like its a no-brainer.

"Just checking. I won't kill my mom. You know, underneath the demon that's taken over is my mom. I love her."

"I know you do," he answers. His voice is soft like a gentle caress, and I feel the hollowness in those words.

"The next few days aren't going to be easy, but I'll let you go to school and check in with the Hendersons. This is top secret," Phantom says.

I nod my head against his chest.

"We have two hours before I let you go. We have to utilize our time so you get the most out of it. First on the agenda: levitation."

I nod again and we enter this dark room. Lights immediately flicker on and there's an empty gym room. Instinctively I press myself closer to Phantom's body.

"Change to Chaos," he whispers in my ear. I shiver against his minty breath and change.

"How did I not realize it? I suspected you were Chaos but there was never proof. You are amazing at hiding your trail, Chaos."

I took that as a compliment.

Chapter 12

My attempts at levitating were not holding out well. Phantom keeps laughing at me when I fall on my backside, the linoleum floor snaking my butt painfully. I wince and get back up on my feet as he laughs so hard that Phantom gasps for breath.

I glare at him, "It's definitely not funny, you know!"

He pokes his tongue out at me and I answer back by scrunching up my face at him.

"Hot," he says with his tone saturated in sarcasm. I roll my eyes at him and motion for him to begin whatever he has planned, knowing full well the training isn't going to end in my favor.

I groan and roll my eyes, "Can we just start the actual training now? I feel like you brought me here just to tease me."

Phantom smirks and I can tell that he's enjoying this about as much as I am loathing it.

"You'll begin by starting on your form." he motions towards a heavy bag that dangles off the ceiling in the far left corner of the gym, "Punch it."

Before I can help myself, I laugh, "You want me to punch? I know how to already!"

Phantom shakes his head of black hair, his long bangs flopping against his forehead, "But you can have more power in those feeble punches if you rotate your hips with the swing. Just a tweak makes things better," he explains like he is talking to a toddler. I should be upset over his tone but I let it slide. Besides, there's no telling what Phantom would make me do if he gets mad and I like my body not being the consistency of Jello.

I march over to the heavy bag and begin punching it, swinging my hips with the motion of the punch. The bag jolts backwards and I step to the side, punching it again as it swings towards me.

"Don't over rotate your hips! If you do that then for a split second you're facing away from the enemy which gives them a chance to attack you," Phantom advises.

I feel so stupid training with him. My cheeks fill with crimson as I do what he says. Phantom seems to be all knowing, but I know how to defend myself and fight people. Heck, I've even knocked Phantom out twice!

"I am not weak!" I grunt as my fist connects with the bag.

"Never said you were," he replies honestly. That comment makes me feel a little bit better about training with him.

"Yeah, you only implied it," I huff.

Phantom tells me to stop and he struts over so that his body is behind mine. He places his hands on my hips and my mouth goes dry. "Don't over rotate," he stresses, his hands forcing my hips to turn a little bit. "That is as far as you need to go. Don't get careless," he warns.

I nod, calculating the degree to turn my hips as his thumbs brush my sides. I try to ignore the feeling that touch gave me as my heart beats in double time and I blush for a completely different reason.

Kelsey Jerrs usually never blushes.

Usually.

I punched the bag for a few more minutes until Phantom got bored.

"Much better. Now we can practice your self defense since I know you suck lollipops at that. Try not to bruise your forearms while blocking this," he suddenly lunges forward and brings his elbow up to hit me in the face. I bring my arms up to shield me from his attack and as Phantom's elbow collides with my arm, pain blossoms.

"Ow!" I cry, stepping away from him to check out my arm. He used his full strength and my arm throbbed.

"I told you not to bruise yourself!" Phantom tsks.

I shoot him a dirty look, "You're the one who elbowed me! How the freak is it my fault?" I exclaim.

"Because you suck at defending yourself. I imagine you get lots of ugly bruises from fighting crime all the time. And by ugly I mean that bruises are hideous to most of the population but for me they're a real turn on. Do you have any bruises?" he raises an eyebrow at me.

My mouth gapes open, "You're disgusting!"

He winks, "Only you make me this way honey."

I gag and before Phantom draws one of his long legs back to kick me. Before his fancy dress shoes can collide with my ribs I catch his shin in my hands and pull him off balance. He falls, turning intangible before he can smack the floor.

"Suck on that juice box!" I yell loudly as I release his leg.

I can hear Phantom's laugh before he pops his head out from the floorboards. I breathe a sigh of relief over the fact that he isn't upset that I have just one-upped him.

"Not bad but you could have been smoother at unbalancing me," he notes.

I stare at him blankly, "What do you mean by that?"

His green eyes pierce mine, "When you made me fall you lost your own footing. Keeping your stance is key when you're fighting someone. Call it luck that I didn't shift my own weight to make you fall over with me. I do love when our bodies connect with each other," he smirks.

I wrinkle my nose up at him in disgust, "Stop with your innuendos. I know you like me," I scoff.

One of Phantom's gloved hands grasps the front of his button-down shirt, "What I say are not innuendos, my dear Chaos."

I put my hands on my hips, "Then what the heck are they?"

He smiles a rare, real smile, "Promises."

"Excuse me?"

He sighs and rolls his eyes at me, "When you finally admit that you love me as much as I love you, then everything I say will happen to you. I always say what I intend to do, Kelsey Jerrs."

A shiver runs through me and I take a few steps backwards as a subconscious way to save myself from his next attack- the two, palm sized green orbs of energy resting in both of his hands.

Phantom's left hand arcs upward as an uppercut. I narrowly avoid it, my hand grasping his and I direct it into the wall nearby. It shreds the wall and his right hand arcs in the same motion, but I know that he doesn't use the same strategy twice in a row.

At the last moment, Phantom brings his knee up to my stomach, making contact. The force of the blow has me flying across the gymnasium floor, and into the roped of a full-sized boxing ring. My limbs get tangled into the ropes and I hang upside down, much to my dismay.

I'm pretty sure the noise that came out of my mouth sounded very strange, I think to myself. How embarrassing!

Phantom floats over towards me, "You didn't block."

"Oh reallllly? Forget Benedict Cumberbatch- you should be the next Sherlock Holmes!" my tone is dripping with venomous sarcasm. The pain in my stomach is worse than my arm. I'm pretty sure he hit my large intestine directly, and it was not happy.

"I hate mysteries," Phantom says just as sarcastically as I did.

"My stomach hates you right now."

He lifts his shoulders in a shrug, "So long as your heart loves me, I think I'll be alright."

I gag again, trying to untangle myself from the ropes. Blood rushes to my head due to my uncomfortable pose and to my horror Phantom helps get my legs untangled while I work on my arms.

"Your hair is a haystack," Phantom comments. "Is that what your bed head looks like in the morning?"

I dust myself off, happily standing on my own two feet, "I don't know. Why would you care?"

The corners of his lips twitch up for a split second, "Fantasies."

I gawk at him silently. My mouth opens to say that he is a piece of work but nothing comes out so I snap it shut. Phantom fantasizes about me? What thing about me is so worthy of that?

"You're joking," I deadpan.

A laugh escapes his lips, and it is as cold and sharp as ever. "If the fact makes you uncomfortable then you can ignore it," he sings.

I push on one of his broad and toned shoulders- not that he budged even an inch, "Why the crap do you have this sick infatuation with me? I am Kelsey Jerrs from the freaking Dumps who has only a blanket and a small handgun to my name! If it wasn't for the Hendersons I would be homeless or dead! You are insane for liking me. I am insane for letting you get feelings for me. Why me when you can have any girl you feeling want? You know what, I am going home. Anna must be off her rocker with worry since I didn't tell her where I was going this morning-"

Phantom's lips collide with mine harshly. His lips force mine to move against his even though I was caught completely off guard that I froze. My mind cannot form a single coherent sentence as his hands grip my waist tightly, fingers digging through my clothes and into my flesh. Right into the few extra pounds of padding I have.

I stiffen and Phantom kisses me harder. Those extra pounds have helped you be a superhero I chant to calm myself down. They are necessary to the superhero life. Other girls would completely agree with me on this.

He bites my bottom lip and I have read enough Young Adult Romance novels in my life to know that he wants full access to my mouth. As if! I shake my head and he growls, pulling away for a breath.

"You are frustrating me, and not the kind your pure little mind conjures when I say frustrating, but the more... intimate kind," he tells me, running both of his hands through his black hair. We look so alike that the resemblance is scary.

I gulp, "Well I don't do alfalfa kisses, Mister!" I yell in my own defense.

Phantom burst into a fit of giggles. Actual giggles that sound like Mrs. Henderson's expensive china breaking.

"Alfalfa? Did you just call French kissing- Holy Rolos that is rich. You are so- I cannot even deal with you right now."

"I'm terribly sorry to burst your bubble but the idea of swapping spit with you is not something I would wish to do. In fact, young battling anyone is really disgusting," I say.

He give me a look like I am completely insane as his shoulders shake with laugher. Phantom's body crouches down and he laughs and laughs.

"What? I have a perfectly normal view on the subject!"

"Bullcrap," Phantom says, desperately trying to pull himself together.

I stare at him strangely, "Well, I'm gonna go home now. I don't know why you kissed me, but it made things awkward. Let's call it a day shall we?"

Phantom looks at me and agrees, which is a rare occurrence.

"BTW, your kissing needs a little more work," Phantom chimes. It isn't meant to be mean and I don't find anything hurtful about his comment.

"You can fantasize about training me how to kiss tonight, Phantom," I say as I open the front door to the Henderson home. The sun is close to setting and I remember the pile of homework I have.

"Take care of your bruises, Miss Jerrs," he advises before disappearing into thin air.

"Will do," I mumble under my breath.

Chapter 13

My muscles ache as I slowly trudged forward through the lawn of the front yard of the Henderson's home, cursing Phantom's name under my breath as I did so. It wasn't fair that he dumped me in front of the bakery he is so obsessed with. After interrogating me if I had taken his recommendation seriously, he wanted to hear all about what I got and if they liked it or not. I had to just walk away from his crazy questions and the way he was antsy for my approval was like a small child doing something to make their parents proud. It was so strange to see.

It had to be after eleven O'clock as I slip the key into the front door and turn the lock. All of the lights inside are off which is normal once Mr. Henderson went to bed. I don't think much of anything as the door creaks open and I step into the foyer. Out of habit, my eyes slide to the chalkboard and I see that Mr. Henderson is staying overnight at the office and Mrs. Henderson is with him. Anna's line is blank so I figure that she is asleep downstairs, and must have turned off all the lights.

Since I am bathed in complete darkness after shutting the front door behind me, I pull out my phone and turn on the flashlight app so I can find my way. I've memorized the layout of the mansion, but want to save myself from stepping on things I shouldn't. I descend the staircase to find that the downstairs lights aren't on either, which should have been a warning sign because Anna likes to leave the bathroom light on when she sleeps. I open the door to her room and call out her name but don't get a reply. Flipping on the lights, I find out that she isn't in the room. A frown appears on my face as I begin to wonder what the heck is going on. If nobody was home why were all the lights off?

I carefully climb the spiral staircase all the way to the master bedroom, using the flashlight to guide me, and see that the french doors are wide open.

Those french doors are always shut. I creep by the large bed which was untouched from when someone made it this morning. Something isn't right...

And that is when it struck me like a jolt of electricity. Nobody was home, which never happens. The lights are all of, which never happens unless somebody was home. But someone is in the house, that is a no-brainer. That person just isn't a Henderson.

I have a pretty good guess as to who it could be. As I turn around, my suspicions are confirmed.

"Crap. I should have seen this coming," I mutter.

She stared at me with black eyes. Even the whites of her eyes are black, and they have been that way ever since I can remember. She wears a faded orange jumpsuit and there are remnants of handcuffs encircling both of her wrists, though the middle chain is broken. Her long black hair that goes to her hips is quite the mess, and a devilish smirk is plastered onto her face.

It's my mother, Maine Jerrs. Of course it is. Who else in this world could it be? Well, besides Phantom.

"Why didn't you come visit your mommy?" Maine asks. The thing about her voice is that it's this high-pitched soprano that is equivalent to a five year old. She always whines, even while stating a fact and it drives me bonkers.

Clenching my teeth together, I grind out, "I was but I got held up. You're freaky if you keep making your daughter play dangerous games. That's why you got locked up for child abuse, in case you have forgotten."

Her pink lips pull into a pout that is dainty and cute... if it isn't for the fact that a forty-nine year old is doing it. I glare at her, meeting her black eyes dead on with my icy look.

"What detained you?" she whines, her interest turning to the doorframe. Maine runs her index finger down the length of the wooden frame as an attempt to look at everything but me. I have a 'nasty glare' that makes her nervous- one of the many reasons she has tried to kill me for.

A smile threatens to be released, "Phantom did. He said that you'll try to kill me, but I know better. Phantom doesn't know how your mind works as much as I do, and I know for an absolute fact that you want me to play your game too much. So much, that it overpowers your killing urges. Of course I also integrated the fact that your trigger hand is clenched tightly into a fist when I made that calculation."

Maine's face twists into a very pissed off look that doesn't really look so good on her. She hates when I get all mathematical on her, or even use my brain around her.

The thing about Maine is that she is not my mom. That's my mom's body, and her rare proud smiles that sometimes break through when we fight, but it's not actually her. She's possessed by an evil demon that has no right to be there. The demon took her over when I was little enough not to remember, yet old enough to take care of myself. Dad had just disappeared, along with my memories of him which is really strange and Mom was sad all the time. I didn't even know that demons existed, but one day she just started to get very angry, and broke a lot of things. That was the first time the demon took her over.

The demon is violent, and loves to create bloodbaths. Luckily, my mom is somewhere in her own subconscious so she isn't aware of anything, which is both a blessing and a curse because if she isn't aware then there is no hope to save her. Many heroes have tried to stop her, but the demon loves pain and loves to utilize it's borrowed body as leverage.

"You locked me up in that cryo tube! I didn't even get a cell or a padded room!" Maine hisses.

I shrug, "Even I can escape a jail cell and a padded room. I figured that if I can do it, then you can do so as well."

"Maybe I should kill you after all," she ponders.

"Maybe I think dying right now would be a drag and would fight you on it," I countered.

"You are a piece of trash, you know that?"

I smile at that, "I am told that at school, but if I'm trash then what are people like you? Dirt?"

And then she lunges towards me. I sidestep into a night-stand and jump over it as Maine's foot lashes towards me.

"You should listen to your mother and play the games. Or you should be nice to your mother and let her kill you!"

I frown because neither one of those options seem like a good idea to me. "I would respect my mom, except you aren't her!"

She yanks on the front of my shirt, effectively stretching it out, "That mouth of yours-! Why can't you just shut up for once in your friggin' life!"

"Sorry, it's a survival mechanism in a half-baked effort of self-preservation. I will attempt to tone it down in the future if you would like," I apologize sarcastically. I should have rolled my eyes as well, but I like living life, and was curious about Phantom's romantic inclination towards me too much to die at that exact moment. Shaking her off, I back into the wall and smooth down my shirt with a light sigh.

"Aw, is Mommy such a bother to you? Do you want me to leave you alone?" Maine taunts in the whiney voice.

My green eyes bore into hers as I slowly shake my head, "Just finish up with why you had to come here in the first place. There are too many authorities looking for you right now for you to be staying in one place too long. I'm surprised that an officer hasn't already shown up at the front door, to be honest. I love cops, they have perfect timing too, sensing something fishy before anyone opens the can of sardines. I consider most of them as my friends, so for once let me tell you something very slowly, because I am serious: Kill a cop and I will hunt you down and throw your demon backside in the Hole of Hell. Do you understand?"

Maine freezes, and then she slowly laughs a humorless laugh that makes me wince more than anything, "I accept your challenge but only if you accept to be my pawn in this game of cat and mouse."

That catches my interest, "Cat and mouse?"

She rolls her eyes and looks at me like I'm the dumbest person in the room, "You don't think that I don't have a target, or an endgame, do you?"

I figure she does, but I shake my head and hope that she'll tell me more. She doesn't though, and had an all-knowing smile aimed in my direction. I clench my teeth together and try to conceal my annoyance.

"You need to leave. Anna's curfew is midnight and it's getting close if you're expecting to saunter out the front door," I say rather rudely. At this point I don't care. She knows that I cannot take her in a fight, so I wouldn't be the one who started fighting her.

"Anna... Are you two still friends? Even though you came from the Dumps, so I thought she would coddle you too much. Do you like being a charity case for the Hendersons?"

I growl, "I am not a charity case! You're just jealous because while I get to live in a mansion, go to school, and actually have a life, you are stuck without any of that. You'll never know true joy because the police will find you if you finally settle down someplace, and you will never find someone who loves you, because who the crap could ever love a killer?"

She doesn't even take any offense to what I say. Instead, she turner out of the room, and walks slowly down the stairs. I notice that her bare feet are cut up on the bottoms and feel kind of sad about that. The orange jumpsuit looks hideous because it gives her a saggy butt, however that part can't be helped.

"Don't tell anyone I visited," she states while opening the front door.

"I won't," I promise. It's true that I won't because the only person i would tell is Anna and she doesn't need the extra stress.

"Oh wait," I call out before she could step outside. "Do you know who wants Anigirl? Someone is targeting her, someone who is supposedly extremely dangerous. More dangerous than you."

She only smiles, "Play the game to find out. I will visit again, Kelsey. You don't know the rules of the game quite yet because I am still setting up the game board. Be patient, honey. Everything will come with time, if you let it."

And them Maine disappears into the night. I stare at the front porch for a few moments, letting out a sight of relief. My shoulders relax and I unclench my fists.

She didn't even attempt to kill me. That only means she didn't want me dead because she needed me. No, she didn't need me, she needs something from me which is completely different.

It made me expendable. And that is when I got scared.

Chapter 14

It wasn't long before I had to go back to school. Even with everything that has been happening, I wanted the only piece of normalcy that I could still have. I knew that Maine would never touch me on campus, since the security is bulked up so much that one could call it excessive. It seemed to me like everyone knew that the villains were planning something sinister, so everyone was on alert. Some parents didn't want their children to attend the academy without a taser and pepper-spray which was hard on the school higher-ups because tasers weren't legal on the academy grounds. It seemed like everywhere I was, there was always someone staring at me. Someone who I couldn't see, and that made me wonder if Phantom was keeping tabs on me or if Maine was. Can't say I liked either of those options, but if I had to pick, I would want Phantom to hang around me.

English begins and we begin the class long discussion on Macbeth and the insanity before the major test tomorrow.

Girl 1 and 2 gossip about the Cardinale family like they always do, and so I catch up on the latest gossip.

"You know, the family has six people living in their house, but the headlines read that the Cardinale's only have five sons."

"Whaaat? That would mean one of the Cardinales is an imposter!" Girl 2 cries.

"That's the thing, all of those boys are real Cardinales. I looked online though, and according to Wikipedia, Emerald Cardinale is actually a cousin. Talk about drama."

"No way! Isn't Tera dating him?"

This causes my interest to pique. I grin evilly as I realize that Tera's plan to join the Cardinale family in marriage could backfire.

"It makes sense, because Emerald is always so moody and handsome. He has weird hair too, it's not blonde like the rest of the boys' are. Of course I wonder why the media had never picked up on it, since I'm sure there is a huge story with an amazing headline waiting to be written on it," Girl 1 states, and I remember that she wants to be a newscaster when she graduates.

"Did you hear about Fern? The klutz literally ran into Jonah Cardinale- who's twenty-nine years old BTW- and apparently he really likes her now. Talk about ew. It makes me want to throw up."

I turn around and look at Girl 2 for a long time. She stares back until I realize that I am staring at her and quickly look away.

"Freaky Gothic loser," Girl 2 mutters loud enough for me to hear. I face the person participating in the class discussion so that I don't have to worry about them.

"I heard that Jonah and Fern made out downtown in the coffee shop. There's pics online but I haven't seen them yet. In fact, I don't want to see ugly Fern with such a beautiful man. It might make me-"

"Girls, I would appreciate it if you three actually added to the discussion. What we are talking about is actually quite relevant to your book final," Miss Benson states sternly. I mash my lips together because I was paying a little attention, yet I still got called out. Hashtag my life.

But the girls promptly shut up, so I was able to even comment a few times during the remaining time of class. When the bell rings, I breathe a sigh of relief but before I can gather all of my belongings into my backpack, Miss Benson slides over to me in her tall wedge sandals. I look at her curiously, and blink a few times.

"I have a favor to ask of you, Kelsey," she begins with a pause in the middle. "Could you keep tabs on Fern for me? Just for a little while until the gossip stops spreading."

I blink a few times as I process this favor, "Why?"

"Well, Jonah really likes Fern and I don't want Fern to get hurt. I know she looks up to you, so give her positive words of encouragement. I know how she feels, and she knows that I'm here for her if she needs anything, but I don't think Fern will take me up on my offer of assistance. Can you just quietly show her support?" she asks.

I shrug, "I don't know what you mean, but whatever. I can say something nice to her in the hall. Well, better go, I really don't want to be late for Pre-Calc."

She nods, a small smile on her face as I stuff my notebooks into my bag and rush to class. I keep my eyes peeled for Fern, but don't see her.

Pre-Calc goes by quickly. I hadn't had time to learn this chapter beforehand like I usually did because I absolutely love math and got impatient when the teacher would spend a few days on the same technique, so I paid attention and actually took diligent notes. We got the assignment- a FUN-sheet packet due on Friday- and I finished the first three pages effortlessly. Numbers just make sense to me, I can't ever explain it.

When the bell rings, I get up, and take the long way to my next class in an attempt to find Fern. My black skirt drags softly against the pavement, and paired with a black long-sleeved scoop neck shirt and a few long emerald neck-laces.

A freshman bounces up towards me, a finger looping around my necklace, "Is this real emerald?" she asks.

I tell her that I wouldn't know since I got it in a bookstore and that it probably isn't. The girl frowns and pulls away, "Well, that's a shame. I wanted to buy it off of you since Emerald Cardinale must like emeralds and my Dad works as his PR assistant."

A teacher walks by and does a double take as he realizes that I am not in uniform. To be honest, I never really am, since the handbook states specifically "Students are allowed to wear black as a symbol of mourning" so whenever I feel Goth that is what I say. Usually, I get sent to the office, but the lady at the front desk is really nice. She knows that my mom is in jail and that my dad is somewhere unknown so she let's me off by writing a note.

I dig in the front zipper of my bag and pull out one note from a few weeks ago, handing it to the teacher. He frowns as he reads it, and then walks away without saying anything, taking the note with him. I huff and head to class, now noteless.

Lunch rolls around and I sit next to Anna immediately. She pulls out two peanut butter and grape jam sandwiches and hands one to me. "Tera is being unusually freaky today," she notes, angling her head towards where Tera is sitting on top of the table, her long, shiny smooth legs stretched out in front of her. I make a face and turn around. Yes, she is even more dolled up than usual, the sleeves of the uniform's white buttoned-down shirt rolled up nicely to her elbows, more makeup smothered on her face, and black stilettos that have very pointy heels.

"Why?" I ask, feigning boredom but actually really wondering about it.

"She's dating a Cardinale, so that must be why," Anna says uninterestingly.

I nod, "Have you heard about Fern and Jonah- of all the people!"

Anna's long brown hair shakes as she nods that she has heard about that subject matter already.

"Have you seen Fern at all today? I haven't, and she must be getting made fun of a lot because she looks very nerdy and not a lot of people would think that a Cardinale would be into a nerd. I mean, I'm okay with it, as long as Jonah makes Fern happy and vice versa!" I say quickly, trying not to sound too mean.

"People have been calling her really mean things today, but Fern is actually taking it very well."

I frown at that news, and then remember that Maine visited me, and I am keeping that a secret. I chew on my bottom lip. Why does my life have to be so dramatic all the time? I wonder frantically. Can't a girl get a break?

Phantom thinks I'm hot, Maine wants to use me for something sinister and then kill me, Miss Benson wants me to be kind to a nerd, and Anna needs me to protect her from the unknown evil villain that wants to kill her or use my best friend for something even more scary.

I can't get a break!

As I bite into the sandwich, I finally see Fern with her bushy red hair and her large glasses balancing on her small button nose. She could actually be pretty, if her glasses shrunk or she got contacts, and her hair grew out a little longer so it wasn't five inches away from her face in pure volume. Her uniform is nicely pressed and her black Converse adds an edgy street appeal. Chewing on my bite, I wave her over and she comes.

"Anyone who calls you anything mean, tell me and I will punch them to the moon. Okay, Fern?" I state seriously.

She smiles, her taunt shoulders relaxing, "Thank you Kelsey! I'm okay though. Jonah said that this would happen the moment he helped me up last night. It will go away just like it did with Ms. Benson.

I smile at her optimism, even though Ms. Benson still had hate mail sent to her, and death threats. It never really goes away, but if that was what Fern wanted to believe then I would rather swim in a dirty lake than to pop her balloon. Anna knows how much I hate lakes. They're too slimy and green for me.

As Fern walks away towards the exit of the cafeteria, I yell, "Where are you going?"

Fern turns around, and her smile brightens so much it blinds my Gothic mood, "To the office," she replies simply before leaving.

I knit my eyebrows together, and look towards Tera to see that she too is gone. Questioningly, I look at Anna who shrugs, "Don't look at me like that. I have no idea what is so important in the front office," she says icily.

I humph and wonder if it was a coincidence or not.

Most likely not.

Turning to fully face Anna I say, "Why don't you pack up your lunch and let's go see what is so great about the front office?"

She gives me a flat look and opens a bag of celery sticks. That would be a no.

I bat my eyelashes a few times, and give her the wide puppy dog eyes that I know must look comical with my charcoal eyeliner and black clothes. Anna laughs at me, and stuffs our food in the bag, "But you have to at least finish off your PB&J before sleuthing, Sherlock."

So I eat that sandwich without breathing and stand up, "Let's go!" I usher with a full mouth.

Anna stares at me, giving me a 'you're completely bonkers but I'm just as curious' look.

And we leave.

Chapter 15

Anna and I slip through the big metal doors of the back of the front office. Attendance supervisors are sitting at their desks trying extra hard to look important when really they aren't. I look around, my black hair falling over my shoulder and blocking half of my view. I take her arm and lead her towards the front desks and sure enough there were a crowd of people. There are four desks lined up, the first two were dealing with the mass of people. I head towards the back left, to Mrs. Shamu. Her last name isn't really Shamu, but it has at least seventeen characters and is not English so it's extremely hard to pronounce.

She eyes my choice of clothing and smiles, pulling a pad of paper towards her and clicking her pen open against her cheek- a strange thing she does- and begins to scribble down another dress code pass for me. I smile and take the note. Anna shakes her head and I smile at her, making use of the excuse for me to check out all the people up front. Fern is there, standing next to a man in a nice suit so I guessed it was a Cardinale boy. And of course there was Tera hanging off the arm of who I guessed was Emerald. Lastly, Ms. Benson is holding hands with Hayden.

I turn back towards the desk, "Thank you so much. Mr. What's-his-face took my other one. The big bully," I release a depressed sigh because I gotta sell the mourning girl act.

Mrs. Shamu tuts and shakes her head, "Some people don't understand the process of losing loved ones."

I turn back to Anna and smirk. She shakes her head at me, her eyes saying a thousand sentences about how she isn't happy that I didn't wear my uniform today.

Tera's glittery necklace catches my eye, and I glance at it. Unfortunately, this action doesn't escape her notice, and she promptly gives me the finger, "Freak off somewhere else!"

My smirk turns as evil as Phantom's as I turn to face her. Anna reaches for my forearm to retrain me. I drag her over to Tera, "Hello Fab Queen!"

Tera growls at me, and I glance towards Emerald, "That's not very attractive, you know. Growling makes you seem more animalistic than you already are and trust me, it's not a good look."

She bares her perfectly white and straight teeth at me, but doesn't say anything. Anna tugs on my arm to leave the office but I ignore her and frown, "Aren't you going to introduce us? No? Well, I'm Kelsey Jerrs and this is my sexy, butt-kicking sidekick Anna Hendricks. We are the official outcasts of this school. I would offer you my autograph, but I have issues with Bic pens and that's all the front office carries in those mugs."

Anna scoffs at that, and Emerald laughs. Finally, someone gets my humor.

"Outcast seems about right," Tera tries to counter.

"I'm not!" Anna defends.

I nod, "Okay, well I'm the only outcast, but that is because I am mourning- something meanie buttocks over there isn't helping with," I say, pointing at Tera.

Tera scoffs, "You're parents are in the Dump's Trash Can. Not my fault they're freaks like you."

I put a hand over my heart and gasp at her outrightness, "Actually they're in jail. C'mon Tera, say it with me: Jail. J-A-I-L. It just happens to be located in the Dumps."

"The Can!" Tera insists. I back off, a smile toying on my face.

"Hey Kelsey!" Fern bounces up to me and reaches for my hand. I give it to her, a look of disgust on my face from the contact. Not that I have anything against Fern, it's just that she's very easy to forget about, and is kind of a nerd. Girls like me don't hang out with nerds.

Anna saves me from responding with a cheerful, "Fern! Long time no see! How is that car repair shop going? I think one of my drivers took Kelsey's van down there yesterday."

I perk up, "What? When? Who took Jorge without me knowing?!" I thought I parked it at the mall for the whole day.

Then the principal waltzes in from his office, "The Cardinale family! What a pleasure it is to see you here this beautiful afternoon. I hope it wasn't a nuisance coming to view the new art studio and this year's gallery?"

"Yes, don't worry about us, Principal Reeves, we have Ms. Benson to guide us around," Hayden's low voice boomed.

I sigh and look over at Ms. Benson's half-moon glasses. I swear they are fakes since she stares over them all the time. She would look younger with contacts, I think.

The Principal looks at me, taking in my appearance, "Miss Jerrs, I am pretty sure we discussed you're uniform already."

I bite my lip and stare at my shoes, "Yes we have. Today is a momentary relapse of judgement."

Anna nudges my shoulder and I glare at her once Principle Reeve's back is turned. He doesn't really care, but those words were a warning for me that next time I'm out of uniform then I'd get sent home.

The bell rings, signaling the end of lunch. I feel Anna stiffen at my side because she is on the opposite side of where she needs to be. I laugh and push through the mass of people to the front door.

"Note to self, do not visit the art gallery anytime soon," I say turning around to look at a stressed out Anna. My smile fades as I keep walking down the hall.

"What's-" I begin, but I slam into something hard. I whip forward and take a step backwards. "Ahhhh! I'm sorry! I really should look where I'm going! Sometimes I don't and that's not good because stuff like this happens and- Oh."

The boy is hot. I'm talking edgy, tight, black leather pants with a graphic shirt that had a palm tree and the works 'You Suck' on it. His white blonde hair is short on the sides but his bangs hang in his face...

...Just like Phantom's.

My eyes are quite possibly the size of saucers as I take in the boy standing before me. We both have the same sharp green eyes with a glint of hatred in them and I knew. My heart leapt out of my chest and I instinctively reach out to grab his black wool jacket. My fingers slide against the fabric but I can't hold onto it firmly enough. As he slips through my fingers, Anna tugs on my arm, leading me in the exact opposite direction. "We're gonna be late!" she stresses.

I spare a glance back at her. "Go on without me," I say, turning back to the boy but of course he was gone even though his figure should have still been strutting down the hallway. I jog to the end of the hall and peer over the corner for any sight of him. It is useless since he is obviously gone, but as I stand by the corner at the end of the hallway I can't help but feel crushed. People bump into me and shoot me nasty glances as I just stand there frozen.

As the last bell rings and the hallway empties I still stand there, staring down the hall. Why was Phantom here? What did he want at my school? Was he here to protect Anna?

So many questions run through my head as class surely begins. I hear the creaking of a security man riding his bike towards me and I slip into the empty library, choosing to brace the wrath of the librarian instead of the security.

"Do you have a pass?" the librarian asks. Her eyes narrow slightly as she notices that I don't have a paper in my hands.

"Nope," I state, popping the 'P' at the end.

"Then you can't be in here," she says in a monotone voice.

"Oh. Then I'll be going to class then," I say, turning around. Before I can take a step out, the lady clears her throat. I square my shoulders and turn back around, "Yes?"

She holds up a pink slip, "You aren't in uniform."

I bite my bottom lip to stop the words I so desperately want to say from coming out. I walk over to the front desk and take the note then head back to the exit, crumpling the paper in my hand and tossing it into the empty trash can next to the doors.

"Excuse me!" the librarian yells as I walk away. I hear her heels clack after me and I duck into another hall and run towards my class.

"Young lady!" she yells as I yank open the door to class. I look over my shoulder and see her walk past the corridor I am in and I step inside the class. The teacher stops mid sentence and reprimands me for being late once again, but as long as the librarian doesn't know where I am I consider myself to be good.

I take my seat in the front row and think about anything but science. Who could think about the lecture when they have seen the #1 hottest villain's identity? An identity that is extremely good looking, by the way. Not this girl, that is for sure.

Feeling eyes boring into the back of my head, I turn around to see the culprit. In the back of the class is that boy, the black sweater slung over the back of his chair revealing a Muse T-shirt and his lips are twisted in a sinister half smile.

Frantically, I turn back to the teacher. Shouldn't he notice that there's an extra student in the back row? I look behind me again and the boy is gone, but the chair is also invisible. I smirk, my eyes narrowing to slits. When we turn invisible, so does everything we touch, I sing in my head.

The teacher slams a textbook on my desk, making me jump, "Miss Jerrs, the PowerPoint is this way," he says pointing to the front of the class.

I turn around and nod, "Yessir."

"You've already interrupted my lesson twice, do not let it happen a third time," he warns.

"Sorry," I say hoarsely.

The class laughs and then the teacher keeps talking. After a few minutes I look back again to see that the chair is visible, but Phantom is gone.

Chapter 16

Anna and I race to get to City Hall. There was a news report that a robbery was going to be attempted, and a note was found on the Mayor's desk that someone else was going to try kidnapping the Mayor and his 'cute secretary' tonight as well. As soon as we came home from school, we dropped our backpacks in the hallway, ran down the stairs to change into our hero's uniforms. Getting into a navy blue maxi skirt and a loose tee with a gray skull on it was easy, so I has time to swipe two mini Ben & Jerry cartons for the road which we devoured hungrily before parking Anna's car at a Super Wal-Mart. With my white blonde, and Anna's fiery red hair we definitely stand out. We walk across the street, and I scuff my black Converse on the side of the road as I trip off the sidewalk curb onto the asphalt.

"Graceful," Anna comments.

"I try," I reply dryly.

She pouts her pink lipstick-stained lips, "Don't be mean, I'm just teasing."

I sigh and look at her, "My bad."

Anna nods appreciatively at my curt apology. People gape at us as we causally walk by. I notice there are more Anigirl fans than anything else so I roll with it, "Anigirl, people are watching us... creepsters."

Anna looks at me with an eyebrow raised, "They always stare."

"That's why you insisted on doing your make-up? Because-ow!" someone takes a photo on their phone, the flash blinding my innocent and sensitive retnas. I growl at the woman and shoot her a nasty glare.

Anna elbows me in the kidney and smiles at the woman, "We are off to save the day after Chaos took a nap. She's a little pissy right now."

I frown at that full-out lie. We both came directly after school so what was her angle? "I am never 'a little pissy' Anigirl. I am just always pissed off at everything that lives and breathes. There's a big difference in our two statements in case you didn't know," I correct, aiming that last part towards the woman.

"This is why you aren't in the Top 10," Anna chimes, walking past the woman and pushing through the crowd of specta-tors that gathered to catch a glimpse of us.

"I refuse to conform to our society's ideals! Hence my Gothic nature and my black mood!"

Anna laughs and then we hear the sirens of the cop cars. Instinctively we both flinch and begin to run towards City Hall. The Police Chargers squeal as they park in front of us, creating some kind of attempt of a barrier. I reach for

Anna's hand and turn intangible, running through the cars and officers and dodging hands that reach out in an attempt to catch us. The police men weren't exactly on any of the super's side, however when it came to fighting more dangerous villains- villains a million times worse than Phantom and his Brotherhood- then they usually left us alone. Depending on who the Chief of Police is, some heroes work along with the PDs. They are lucky, because in my town that is not the case.

As we reach the front doors, a SWAT team pulls up, but I dive through the entrance, dragging Anigirl along with me. She breathes heavily, tugging away from my grip and changing into a lioness. She bounds up the stairs to the second floor, ignoring the secretary who calls out to us to stop right here. SWAT members open the door, the wood slicing through me. I shiver as it goes through me, not expecting that movement. Just because I am intangible doesn't mean I don't feel what goes through my body. When I expect it, I brace myself for the feeling, but unexpected things make me feel strange.

I cling up the stairs, my Converse squeaking against the marble tiles awkwardly. I hear Anigirl's roar and the suited up SWAT team follows me. I beckon for them to follow me, "Let's go!" I call.

In a long hallway, I stop being intangible and quiet my footsteps, motioning for the team to do the same. "Hold hands," I order as a precaution. They all look at me strangely and do so, "If there are armed persons in there, then I will make you all intangible. There won't be any death today for any of you. Just trust me." If it comes to me actually making the team intangible, then it would drain my energy. I used a lot for Anna, and I am not sure how long I could hold up if I had to actually make full men share my powers.

I hear a growl, and I kick open the door to the Mayor's office and take in the scene. The Mayor is nowhere to be found.

"Dangit!" I curse. There are two super villains, armed heavily with guns and other forms of weapons. Immediately, the barrel of four pistols is aimed at me heart, making my heart rate skyrocket. They're wearing Brotherhood masks- the organization that Rush and Phantom belong to- but they are too hideous to be Rush or Phantom. Maybe they are copycats? Whatever the case, the fact that they have the red and black masks on is alarming. I stand close to the first SWAT member just in case those guns change their targets.

"Where the frick is the Mayor?" I ask Anigirl but it's not like she can answer. I sigh and turn towards the two men, "Well?"

"The Brotherhood is forever!" they both answer in synch.

I frown, "What does the crappin' Brotherhood have anything to do with my question? Are you retarded or something?" I ask harshly. The sound of four safeties turning off makes me stiffen. The fact that the guns had safeties on in the first place is not a very Brotherhood thing to do.

"Their copy cats!" I cry, running up to one of the masked men and kicking him in the stomach. The SWAT team rushes in, their guns raised. Anigirl moves to take the other man down, but he fights her off. She transforms into a butterfly to get up in the air, and then untransforms, her human body crashing hard into the masked man. A shot gets fired off as I punch my man to the floor, straddle his stomach, and knock him out.

"Where's my Staples button?" I ask Anigirl. She laughs and shakes her head, and then I feel it. The excruciating fire that blossoms on my side.

I drop to my knees, and my hand presses to the source of my agony. Blood. The bullet grazed me. I thank my lucky stars I wasn't actually shot because in my lint of work, getting shot happens a lot of times, and between Anna and I, we have been shot eight times and had to self stitch ourselves up which hurts no matter how many Advil one takes to numb the fire.

Phantom shot me back in the early days. It hit the top angle of my shoulder and I cried. Mortifying as it was, he did give me the best dose of numbing medicine and took the bullet out for me. I still have the scar which is cool but not cool when attempting to wear a black one-piece swimming suit and Mrs. Henderson asking about it. A burn from a cigarette kind of looks the same so that was my excuse, but if she looked closely, it is easy to see the small holes of the stitches.

I apply pressure to the wound and Anigirl helps me stand up. The man I knocked out begins to moan and I kick the side of his face so he shuts up. The move is morbid, cruel, and probably breaks his cheekbone, but he stops groaning so it is worth it.

"Oh my gosh, you got shot!" Anigirl gasps, noticing the blood on my hands.

I grit my teeth and lift my chin up high, "Tell Rush that we have some wannabes. I'm sure he can teach these two kids a thing or two about acting to be in the Brotherhood."

"Woah, bad mood much?" she mutters under her breath. I glare at her. Yes, today hasn't been the best of my Chaos days but I was annoyed at my own stupidity.

"We need to find the Mayor," I grind out between my teeth. I look at the SWAT team, "You can either work with me or get out of my way. Which one?" then I lead them out towards the opposite side of the building that we came through, to the back.

"Chaos?" Anigirl asks. She puts a hand on my shoulder as an attempt to soothe me. She's been touching me a lot lately. What does she know? "The Brotherhood's latest hideout is in the opposite direction."

I give her an empty look, "Who said we are going to the Brotherhood? Why would I lead a SWAT team to that hornet's nest?"

She sticks her lips out in a pout but follows me. The secretary runs up to me, her heels clacking against the marble, "You can't go in there!" she yells grabbing the back of my shirt and twisting it so my lower back is exposed. Luckily for her it wasn't the side where I was bleeding.

"Don't touch me!" I snap.

"Chaos!" Anigirl cries out sternly. She gives me a strange look as I cross my arms over my chest.

"Why can't we go in there?" Anigirl asks, laying the sweetness on a bit thick.

"Because someone very scary is down there," she states hoarsely, her voice barely above a whisper.

I think about my mother. Could she be down there? I but my lip and decide that no matter what, Anigirl can't go down to the basement before I have a chance to first.

"I'll go down first. Since I can be invisible and intangible then I will be the best option. We don't know what is down there except that lady, and I don't want to take risks unless it's under extreme circumstances," I say.

"We go together," Anigirl counters.

"I don't have enough energy to make us both go ghost," I say in my 'that's final' voice.

"Are you PMSing right now or something? Who the crap peed in your Cheerios?" Anigirl grumbles.

My mother, I think to myself, my lips twisting into an almost smile.

"I'm perfectly fine, Anigirl. Just let me go first."

Without waiting for her retort, I turn on my heel and open the door to the dark basement. The stairs creak under my weight and I frown. They aren't very sturdy stairs, but with the tall file cabinets that contain files of who knows what might cushion the blow if I fall through the wood.

Bullets rip through the air, but they all go through me and hit the brick wall behind me.

"That's not cool at all," a voice mutters. I recognize it as Rush, and look to see him grabbing the gunman by the throat, cutting off his airways.

"What if my baby was the one who came down and you shot her? I'd be very upset, kill you, bury your body in the cornfield, then make a point to piss all over your grave every single day. Don't mess with my baby girl," his Jersey accent is prominent as Rush warns the gunman of his impending death.

"Don't kill him," I say, taking the last step.

Rush looks at me, angling his head of curly brown hair to the side, "Why not? I want to rip his vocal pipes out from his throat... it seems like a fun way to die to me..."

I make a face. What does Anna see in someone like Rush? He's scary.

His grip loosens, "Fine. You want to join the Brotherhood? Let me take you to that hellish place! I will be the ferryman for your soul!"

I wince, that was very harsh. At least Rush is open about the Brotherhood, unlike Phantom who is very tight lipped about his whole ties and origins.

Another voice speaks up, "Oh Rush, I didn't know you think that our home is Hell. That makes me very upset."

A chill runs through my spine at the sound of that voice. It's a voice that belongs to my number one person that I never wanted to run into ever again. Let's just say, the last time I heard that voice, Chaos was pronounced dead on multiple occasions while in the hospital.

As his face comes into the light, my heart hammers in my chest and my face pales.

"Aw crap," I mutter as the door opens, and Anigirl pokes her head through the door, getting a view of the super villain in front of me.

Let's just say that Anna said the bad word once she realized what was going on.

Chapter 17

I look at Anigirl and then back to the man that Rush held in a death vice. I couldn't reach her if the masked man let a bullet go. I couldn't be fast enough to save Anigirl.

"Don't you dare look at her!" Rush roared, shaking the man so his attention faced Rush instead of Anigirl.

"The villain's got a soft spot for the hero, eh?" the masked man choked out.

"Darn right I do!" Rush hissed.

"The Brothers will not like that fact... I am doing you a favor, my future brother," the man said, pointing the gin and shooting in Anigirl's vicinity.

I scream and jump up to have my body shield Anigirl's. One thing I am not good at is defying gravity like Phantom is. The bullet doesn't hit either on of us though, but instead gets drilled into the wall.

"What do you want?" Anigirl asks, lowering her voice to that seductive tone she does when she's flirting.

"You crappin' piece of-" Rush begins, pounding the man's back roughly into the wall. "I'm going to tear your limbs off one by one, and then dump them in a trash can!"

"I thought-" the man tries to reply but his breathing gets cut off as Rush's grip tightens around his throat. I step closer to them, trying to get the gun that is in the man's hand. "You were... going to piss... all over my... grave."

"That was before you tried to shoot my baby girl!" he growls. I take another step closer, and then two more without the masked man noticing.

"Only I can rough her up. You touch her, or one of your bullets hit her and you're dead," Rush warns. Chills run down my spine as his voice is dripping with anger and violence.

Anigirl touches my back, letting me know that she has moved from the stairs. I tense but then relax once I realize who it is.

"Don't come closer, Baby," Rush warns.

"Don't kill him yet, Rush. We need answers. Why are his buddies here to kidnap the mayor? Where is he?" Anigirl asks in that low voice.

"It's practice," the masked man replied like he was stating the obvious.

"Practice for?" Rush asks.

"Her," he answers honestly, motioning towards Anigirl.

"Where is the mayor?" Anigirl asks, her voice strong and deep like the man didn't just say that they were going to try kidnapping her.

"He could be dead for all I-" but the man didn't answer because someone appeared, holding an important organ that had just come from the man's torso.

"Ah, so sorry to cut this fun short, but I had an itch to kill and his spleen was calling to me," Phantom says, letting out a long sigh and throwing the spleen onto the floor. The man chokes on his own blood and then begins to jerk. One of his long sleeves of his white button down was rolled up, his forearm covered with blood. It's one of Phantom's signature ways to kill, ripping out organs and then tossing them next to the body.

He looks at me, and the horror on my face because I have never actually seen him do that before and the amount of blood spilling out of the man is making the whole room start to spin.

"He wanted to join the Brotherhood," Rush growled to Phantom.

Phantom kicks the man's body with one of his dress shoes, "In a way he has. The Brotherhood is a lot like Hell I imagine."

Rush laughs, "That's what I said."

Anna sighs, "Can we go get the mayor now?"

"That's kind of important..." I add under my breath.

Rush gives me a look that said to shut up so I bite my bottom lip and do so. Scenarios run through my head about what could have happened to the mayor. He could be dead for anyone knows. First thing first: tell the SWAT team to come follow me.

I started towards the stairs before Phantom grabs my arm with his unbloodied hand, "And just where the crap do you think you are going?" he wonders.

"Up the stairs to the SWAT team that's awaiting my orders," I say rudely. It's none of his business.

"And you think that going alone will be safe even if there are Brotherhood slanderers on the other side of the door?"

"I think it'll be safer for the mayor if we find him quickly, and I can't do that when I am staying in this basement," I counter.

Phantom snickers, "Salty."

I walk up the steps and push open the door. Phantom follows me and when I freeze, he phases his head through my diaphragm to see the view, which was very awkward for me- having a head through my diaphragm is not normal.

"Holy-" Phantom swears as he takes in the dead bodies of both my SWAT team and more masked people.

"What happened?" I whisper, eyeing all the blood on the white marble floor. Those stains wouldn't come out no matter what, since the blood seeped into the cracks and crevices of the marble. Phantom slipped two fingers to a SWAT member's throat, checking for a pulse. By his cheshire grin I figure he is dead and let out a frustrated sigh.

"Why, why, why, why, why!" I yelled. It wasn't a question, but an exclamation of my feelings.

Phantom's smile widened and he began walking to the front door where fifty guns aimed on his heart. He walked through the doors and lifted both of his hands up, "The people who did this are copycats. They took your corrupt mayor who is most likely dead by now. Have fun looking for him, may I recommend beginning the search at the abandoned warehouses or the bottom of the nearest lake?"

I fell to the floor as bullets started to ring out. They didn't hit either of us, but shattered the inside of the Town Hall.

"How rude. Chaos is already hurt. She needs some medical attention ASAP. Only I am allowed to kill her, not some rotten little scumbag."

"That makes me feel good," I mutter.

"Hey Chief!" Phantom raises his voice. I groan because whenever he and the chief of police chitchat, it never ends up good, "Today my favorite song is Muse's Panic Station. You should see the mass of dead bodies in there, it is wonderful! Absolutely special and panic station-y."

The Chief straitened his shoulders, "Today I feel like Twenty One Pilot's Fairly Local."

I bang my head against the marble floor, still crouched as close to the ground as possible, "And I'm an Albatraoz," I mutter.

Phantom must have heard that because he turned to look at me with a strange look on his face, "You would feel like an Albatraoz."

"Why don't you shut up?" the Chief said.

1 "Sometimes quiet is violent," I mutter.

Phantom snickers, 1 "And now I just sit in silence."

The Chief ordered the guns to lower, and he walks over to Phantom, "What happened in there?"

"Mmmm, Chaos and I are having a bit of fun, but I'll tell you this: 2 The normals they make me afraid, the crazies they make me feel sane. Decipher that and you have an answer."

I laugh, and quote, 3 "Maybe it's a cruel joke on me, whatever, whatever. Just means there's way more cake for me, forever, forever."

The Chief stares me down, "This is not your party."

4 "Guess I better wash my mouth out with soap," I grit me teeth as I sit up.

"Can we stop with the Melanie Martinez? There are hundred of other artists, artists who play the electric guitars and also have amazing bass," Phantom pouts.

I check my wound, "I'm sorry you only know one of her songs and feel left out, Phantom. If it makes you feel dead inside, then I'll stop," 5 I tell him.

"That is much better," he replies.

"Shut up both of you and show me what is in there," the Chief demands.

5 "You know you were my oppressor, but now it feels like you are my handler," Phantom mumbles under his breath, opening the remains of the front door to let the Chief in.

5 "I must disassociate from you," I add, taking a few steps away from the Chief.

"Shut up!" the Chief orders, "It's as if you two are toddlers. Aren't you supposed to hate each other?"

5 "His heart is a cold and impassive machine," I whisper to Phantom.

"How come when you quote Muse it makes me want to kiss you?" Phantom groans in my ear. His lips graze the bottom of my ear and I shiver.

"Because the Psycho album is precious?" I try to reply.

Phantom laughs as the Chief takes in the scene that is around him. His face goes a light gray and I become concerned for his health. He isn't exactly young anymore, but his beady eyes have taken in more than I could possibly comprehend.

"These are the copycats?" he asks grimly.

I nod as Phantom answers, "Yeah. But they kill under the name of the Brotherhood which means that if there are any cases where undocumented Brotherhood members are creating destruction then they aren't real. You have the list of us Brothers I assume?"

"Yeah, yeah," the Chief replies.

"They wear these phony masks which is easy to distinguish from the actual masks we like because the glitter in the spray paint can be easily visible through even a grainy security camera. Authentic masks are made with acrylic, not something as cheap as spray paint," Phantom kneels at one of the corpses and takes off the mask with a bullet hole in the forehead.

My stomach rolls at the sight of the person and the gore. It isn't pleasant so I look away and focus on a point on my shoes that could be deemed as interesting.

"Anigirl and Rush are in the basement. We suppose that the mayor was taken by the use of the leftover remnants of the underground railroad tunnels. You can send your men down there and smoke out the mayor and his takers then the Brotherhood will deal with the rest. Take caution, Sir, because if you go in guns a'blazing then you and your men will die," Phantom cautions.

"Then why don't you two go looking first?" the Chief asks.

I laugh, "Why on the planet would I voluntarily go underground with the person who most wants to kill me? Are you insane? No offense," I wince at the venom in my voice.

"True. If we are underground together for a long period of time, I might be tempted to do... things," Phantom agrees. He sends me a look that has raw passion in his eyes. I make a gross face back at him.

"Get a grip on yourselves!" the Chief snaps. We both look at him like he offended both of our great aunts.

"No fun. I was actually wishing for alone time with her," Phantom mumbles.

I gag in a very unladylike manner, "Absolutely not. You have to tie me up and throw me over your shoulder in order to have alone time with me."

I set myself up for the heated gaze Phantom gave me, "That could be easily arranged. In fact," he opens his jacket and pulls out a length of rope from his jacket pocket, "I always come prepped for an opportunity."

I swallow loudly, and shake my head, "No way."

"There's no need," the Chief spoke up. "Take me to the basement now."

Phantom looks at the Chief, "I am not responsible for whatever Rush is doing to Anigirl."

I give him a grossed out look and just shake my head, "Well Anigirl and I will look around town tonight and try to find the mayor, since everyone is more interested in whatever is in the basement." I clear my throat and cry, "Anigirl, let's ditch this crime scene!"

When there isn't a reply, I sigh and figure she's with Rush, "Well I, at least, am leaving. TTFN suckers."

Then I turn my back on Phantom and walk our of Town Hall, my sneakers squeaking against the marble in the silence.

Chapter 18

Immediately after returning from Town Hall, I lay flat on my bed, headphones blasting Panic! At the Disco and my eyes closed. My Pre-Calc homework laid on my chest with a pencil balanced on top of it- not like I am doing it or anything. After staring at the fifth problem for a half hour I finally gave in and stopped trying to think about math. The Mayor had ben kidnapped and that fact doesn't sit well with me. As much as I tried to drown out my thoughts with blaring music, it didn't help.

I hear Anna's steps down the stairs and she knocks lightly on the door of my room before opening it a bit and poking her head through, "How are you?" she mouths when I point to my earbuds.

I sigh, although I couldn't hear myself, "I'm tired."

She smiles and walks over to my bedside, pulling out one of my earbuds, "We failed today. The Mayor was long gone before we even got there. The police are livid that we didn't help but caused major problems. Even the Detectives were upset with me. I had to try my best to smooth things over with them. They were talking about calling heroes vigilantes once again. Kells, I don't want to revert back to the time of Junior High when we both had to sneak everywhere."

"The police have never liked me, Anna," I state, pausing my music and sitting up.

"They don't believe you are good, but that's okay because I know that you are. You just aren't recognized enough."

Because I'm not one of the top 10 supers? I think sourly to myself with an internal groan. "Nothing you say can make me feel better about the Mayor so just go do your homework before it gets to one in the morning and you're sobbing to me for help. I'm tired so I'm going to go to bed soon," I state.

Anna huffs and shoots me her attempt of a glare. It makes me laugh, her blonde eyebrows pulled together make her seem more confused than angry.

"You know, I'm beginning to think that only Phantom is on the same wavelength as you. You two should hang out more," Anna says, grabbing the doorknob.

"Oh... I would but I don't really have his number," I sass.

"L-O-L. You shouldn't have said that," Anna slams the door and then I hear her slam the door to her room with a giggle.

I feel arms wrap around my shoulders and scream, my body tensing. Gloved fingers brush my hair away from my ear, and I can feel his breath on me, "999-888-7777."

A growl escapes my lips, "That's not even a real phone number!"

"Finally, you're out of that dismal maxi skirt and are in tight sweat pants. Makes your butt look fantastic," Phantom smacks my rear end and I jump in his arms.

"Can you not harass me please? You're obnoxious."

He presses his face against my collarbone, still invisible. I feel his smile against my skin, "It's my real number. Girls call me on it all the time."

"It wasn't like I was serious about calling you to... hang out," I but my lip hard to keep myself from smiling, "So you didn't have to give me the digits."

He turns visible, and I see his legs on both sides of mine. He sits against the headboard of my bed, and I check to see his leather clad rear end is snuggled on top of my pillow. Ugh. Talk about disgusting.

"Did I hear you say the word 'digits' when referring to my phone number?" he shudders against my back.

"Did Anna really think it was a good idea for you to be in my room?" I ask but before he can answer I turn around and put a hand over his mouth, "Do not answer that."

His eyes narrow and I feel him lick my palm and I draw it back lightning fast, a disgusted look on my face, "You just licked me!"

He smirks evilly, " When you let me, you won't hate that fact later in our... relationship- I can guarantee that."

It's my turn to shudder at his words, "There is something wrong with you."

"We have already established that fact. Hence why I am a villain."

I huff and lean against him, "I saw you at school."

A gloved finger grabs a lock of my hair and he twirled it around his finger, "Mmm, no you didn't."

"Liar, we have the same eyes no matter what form we are in. Plus, platinum blonde hair isn't so common around here as you might think," I reply in a matter of fact tone.

"Maybe I wasn't there for you but for the Cardinales? That's plausible."

"I don't want to talk to you anymore. It's late and I have," I lift up my worksheet, "Pre Calculus homework."

"Beautiful and a genius. I likey," he teases.

I move around out of his arms on my bed, "When I stated that I was tired, I meant it. You have to go."

"I can stay. There isn't anywhere I need to be at the moment anyways," he moves so we lay together on the mattress. I tense up and he throws the comforter over us.

"Relax," he whispers in my ear. It's impossible for me though since I know that one either his eyes leave me to look at the ceiling he'll see a poster of himself with lots of pins in strategic areas.

I let the worksheet flutter to the floor, "Can you turn off the light?"

I don't feel him move but his body leaves me and the lights turn off before he lays by me on top of the blanket I'm under, our bodies touching at every point. I can feel his calm breathing, "Nice poster. Love the pins on my d-"

I cut him off, "Don't say it!"

"Pee-pee," he finishes against my protest.

Blood rushed to my cheeks and I stare at the wall, "You did not just say pee-pee. Are you five?"

"Only when we're alone. When I'm surrounded by idiots I can somehow manage to act my age," he replies snootily.

"When we're alone you tend to do lots of things," I reply dryly.

One of his legs swing over to rest on mine, "But no sex yet. Interesting."

I open my mouth to respond, my body tensing once again, but then I snap it shut and choose not to respond. If I'm quiet, then maybe I can get a shot of sleeping, I think. It might work if Phantom decides to marvel in the darkness with me. His leg weighs down on me and it makes my feet begin to fall asleep.

"To be honest, I liked the mystery about the girl behind the mask. I could have figured out you were Kelsey Jerrs if I wanted to, but you were too sexy and I knew that you could be a nerd and shatter my dreams about you. Luckily, Kelsey Jerrs is super sexy as well and you do not wear those freaking maxi skirts! How lucky am I? So I want to keep your body a mystery for as long as I can."

"You're assuming that I want to sleep with you, which I can honestly say that I do not," I answer.

"Let me guess, I'll have to put a ring on your finger before-hand, right? I can do that," he trails a finger down the side of my body.

"Is that the only reason you'd propose to me?" I ask.

"What kind of a man do you think I am? Why would I want to marry a toy? Why would I be here right now protecting you if I didn't care for you?" he scoffs, slapping my butt.

I squeeze my eyes shut and think about his words.

"No girl treats me the way you do. We just get each other, and that is what makes being around you, and tormenting you so much fun. Where you're lacking, I have plenty and vice versa. You tame the bloodlust I have, and I make you fired up with all kinds of heat. We are like the pieces of a-"

"If you say puzzle I'll kill you," I spit out venomously.

"-An apple pie," he covers up. "I hate puzzles as well- too many dang corners. Pies are round and perfection. Just like your butt in those pants. Seriously, you're banned from wearing those maxi skirts ever again. Now that I have glimpsed of it, there is no way I can go back."

I bring out one arm from under the covers to elbow him in the chest and he grunts, and then laughs at me, capturing my hand in his.

"You have school tomorrow, yes? Why don't you go to bed?" he teases.

"You're leg is making my legs fall asleep and it kind of hurts," I mumble.

"If you face me I'll set your ensnared legs free," he bar- gained.

I sigh and then turn over, my forehead touching his shoul- der. Phantom places my hand on his chest and I feel his heartbeat through his fancy vest, "So you do have a heart! I have always wondered about that..."

"Without a heart I would be dead," Phantom deadpanned.

"You could be a vampire. That could be why you have insatiable bloodlust and like creating carnage," I muse.

"I create carnage because I get bored. I get bloodlust be- cause I get turned on when people scream. The bloodlust has lost its savor since I met you though. Only the hero can satisfy this villain. Go to sleep."

I grip his vest and close my eyes. It takes a while but before I know it, Phantom hushed up and I fell into a strange sleep.

Hearing a scream, I jolt up in bed. I look around to try to find the source of the scream and realize that I was the one who let it out. Phantom's hands grip the front of my T-shirt which is soaked through with sweat.

"You're okay," he says in an attempt to console me. I crawl over him to stand and turn on the lights. In the mirror by my door I can see clearly that I am definitely not okay. My hair is matted with sweat and poking out in crazy angles and my clothes are drenched. Tear tracks stain my cheeks like I've been crying but I didn't know it.

Phantom's mouth drops to the floor once he sees the state I am in, "I take that back..."

He gets off the bed and walks towards me. I realize that he took off his vest and shirt, his hands don't have those black gloves covering his fingers, and he traded his dress pants for a pair of gray baggy sweats that I got from a White Elephant present so they were huge even on him. Maybe I should have been concerned about the fact he rummaged through my dresser and was wearing girl XXXL sweats but I didn't allow myself to focus on that.

Phantom grips my arms and looks down to meet my eyes, "What happened?"

"I need to rinse off in the shower. I'm gross," I say robotically.

He sighs and I notice a smear of mascara on the plains of his chest. Automatically, I lick my thumbs and rub it off. Phantom stiffens for a moment before he relaxes, his arms falling to his sides, and begins to laugh, "What a mom move you just made."

The lights of the downstairs flicker on and Mrs. Henderson enters my room, "Kelsey? Are you the one who screamed so loudly I could hear it two floors above?"

I look to where Phantom was, but he's invisible so I turn back, "Yeah. Sorry about that."

"Oh dear! You have to shower! You're drenched with sweat!"

"I noticed," I sass, turning to the dresser and pulling out a new pair of sleep shorts and my handy E=MC2 shirt.

Mrs. Henderson groans, "Not your nerd shirt..."

I raise an eyebrow and she catches her mistake, "Don't get your Einstein shorts! Do. Not. I'm good with the math equation one and the red shorts. Cute."

"You should go back to bed," I suggest.

She hesitates, "Are you sure?"

"I'm peachy Mrs. Henderson."

She slowly leaves, poking her head out for a moment longer before shutting the door and heading up the stairs. I wait until I hear the footsteps recede and then I look at Phantom who's now visible, "I'm just going to rinse. It'll be fast so no peeking."

He looks at my shelf of books, "No problem. Mystery, remember?"

I nod and grab my towel before walking to the bathroom and closing the door behind me.

Chapter 19

I open the package at the dining room table. I know exactly what the gift is before opening it, and I know exactly who sent it.

A Metallica album falls out of the package and into my hands. I scream bloody murder, and threw the CD across the room where it thuds against the wall and lands on the floor. My eyes are wide, mouth halfway opened with shock, and my body physically could not move. Terror ices my veins and my body begins to tremble but I know that I am the only one home since Anna really is out with her guys friends.

When I am finally able to come to my senses a little bit, I walk out of the mansion and get into Jorge. The engine takes a few turns to start, and by the time the engine revs Phantom is sitting lazily in the passenger seat.

"This is a crap car," he comments.

"Shut up! Jorge is very sensitive," I grumble, not in the mood to deal with Phantom's bull.

"I heard you scream but I was busy running over some-one's cat. Evil was a priority. Where are you going? I ask because usually you walk or take a cab to wherever you want to go but now you're driving yourself."

I look at him as I pull out of the neighborhood, "I'm heading to the Dumps."

I expect him to be pissed about the fact, but Phantom kicks his boots up on the dash, "Then it's gonna be quite a ride."

Looking ahead I smirk. The CD still plagues my mind and the secret message. Maine gives me Metallica as a warning- a symbol of what is to come. It's a code that I was taught while she raised me. I fear two things in my life- Metallica and apple pies.

Phantom flicks on the radio, and a pop song blasts through the speakers.

When we get to the mall, I park in the back entrance, and hop out. Phantom tags along, his hand gripping the back of my shirt and his body invisible. I can feel the fabric of his glove on my lower back, just above the waistband of my jogging sweats and it makes me uncomfortable but I don't say anything about it.

The place where the city becomes the Dumps is evident. Once I step over the sidewalk, trash litters every single street corner and a rancid smell pierces my nose. I hear Phantom's low cough as he smells it too. My cheeks burn with embar-rassment although there is nothing I have to be ashamed about. Just because I grew up here doesn't mean that Phan-tom would lose interest with me. A man with baggy gangster pants runs past me and pukes on the nearby corner. I gag and cover my mouth and nose with my hand, trying hard not to sympathize with him and puke too. My steps turn into a light jog as I run towards the direction of a dinky apartment complex. The wooden beams are rotted through and the tin eaves that they hold up are close to collapsing. The walls have remnants of the original white paint, although now it looks yellow. The doors have lost their numbers a long time ago, just the shadows of the numbers remain.

"I though you would live farther into the Dumps," Phantom murmured into my ear.

"It's close to the mall, which is why I walk to it," I pant, out of breath from the running.

We both walk up the stairs, which are rotted steel. They creak under Phantom's weight and I snicker. Even if he's invisible, he can't be silent. He smacks my butt so hard I yelp.

"At least I can hover," he grumbles as the creaking stops on the third flight.

I stop and turn in the direction of his voice, rubbing my palm where he hit, "Why do you spank me all the time? It's kinky!"

"It is far from kinky..." he sighs, "Maybe you should look up the word so you can actually use it right. Or would you possibly like a demonstration?"

My mouth dries, "I'm good. Thanks for the offer though."

He chuckles as I finish the stairs and run to the room. I stare at the apartment and I can hear the beginnings of the Metallica CD. My body freezes as the electric guitar strums and the drums work. Phantom turns visible, and he looks at me curiously as the vocals begin. The song skips roughly and I hear the haunting words that should never be sung.

Now I lay me down to sleep/ Pray the Lord my soul to keep/ If I die before I wake/ Pray the Lord my soul to take...

I don't realize that I'm echoing the words with the music until my lips stop moving and the music pauses. She's in there, I realize and I grip the doorknob but it's locked.

"Enter Sandman," Phantom notes.

I nod and kick the door open but Maine is long gone by now, the old boombox blaring Guns 'N Roses. I take a deep breath and walk in. The rooms are still how I remember them. Even the princess dress Maine dyed black was hanging off the back of one of the kitchen chairs. I walk to it and my fingers brush Aurora's face on a plastic button at the heart of the neckline.

"You went hardcore Goth even as a kid?" Phantom asks.

"No, Maine dyed it while I was at school one day. I hated her for a while after that incident. Daddy would call me everyday to make sure I was fine but then I realized that I never had a dad and I... well, I tried everything I could to escape this place."

I know that Phantom gets what I am trying to say. He touches my side where a large stab wound is, and no villain gave me that scar. If it wasn't for Anna's mom, I would probably be dead like I wanted. But looking back, I realized that it wouldn't have been worth it.

My eyebrows furrow and I walk over to the hallway. Yes, there is still the puddle of crimson on the carpet. I wonder idly where the knife went but remember Mrs. Henderson pulling it out of my side and tossing it away.

"Is this your blood?" Phantom asks, crouching next to the red.

I purse my lips, which gives him the answer and he frowns, "Did Maine do that?"

"Wh– Oh no. She didn't stab me."

He looks up, something clouding his eyes, "As a kid, you stabbed yourself? What the– How can someone twist a kid like that?"

"Escape," I whisper quietly.

His eyes show me everything he doesn't let himself say. That he has been there too, and he understood. Maybe not in the same exact way but it is still the same.

"I'm going to kill Maine," he states, his voice lower than I have ever heard it before.

"I'd let you but that stands against everything a superhero believes in."

"Then try to send me to jail afterwards, I don't care. Maine is messed up and she doesn't deserve to head back to her padded cell. She escaped once, she can do it again."

"Exit light, enter night..." I hum as I step over the blood and head down the hallway to my room. It's tiny, only a mattress on the floor and black sheets that are stapled onto the wall so that no sun shone through the window panes. Looking at it now, I can see how twisted the whole apartment it, how twisted my whole childhood was.

"I'm messed up," I murmur, pointing at a teddy bear with the arms cut off. I didn't do that, but I was responsible for the stab marks on the headboard. It was practice.

Phantom leans into me. He wraps his arms around my shoulders and his cheek rests against mine, "I don't think that's necessarily a bad thing."

"I just want this game to stop. I've been playing my entire life and now I am done. I just want to be able to be a normal girl but I realize that being normal is not in my deck of cards life gave me," I confess.

Phantom smiles, "Normalcy is overrated. Life is much better being an abnormality."

That statement brings a small smile to my lips, "I guess so."

"Let's get out of this place. It obviously isn't helping you any to be here."

I consent and together we leave the apartment to head back outside. The sky has turned a dark lavender hue and the clouds seem Gothic. How fitting. I run my hands through my black hair and sigh, walking back to the mall.

"The clouds are pretty," Phantom states, gazing at the sky.

I agreed.

Chapter 20

I park Jorge and immediately know something is up. The front door is open, the glass windowpane shattered like a fist had been through it. I know because I had done the same things many times before– something that came with the superhero territory. Phantom had me drop him off at Crumbles, so he was nowhere to be seen. I get out of the car, and walk towards the door cautiously. My mind wonders if Maine had left and I push against the doorframe to open it more so I can fit through.

"I'm baaaaack!" I yell to nobody except maybe the intruder. I don't know why I state my presence, but it makes me feel better to know that I won't scare the person if he or she is still there.

"Shopping was eventful, but I didn't come back with any-thing," I continue as I pray that I'm just talking to myself an no someone who will try to kill me. "I mean, I saw stuff I liked but it was so expensive even the Cardinales couldn't be able to afford it. That's my luck I guess..." I trail off and walk towards the kitchen, setting my keys down on the counter.

"Kells? Mmm..." A voice grumbled. There was heavy coughing as I look behind the counter to see Mrs. Henderson lying on her side, a trail of blood running down the side of her mouth. There are a few broken tiles on her left and I figure someone smashed her head into the ground.

"What happened?" I gasp, kneeling on the floor to help her. She should not be awake at the moment. Blood trails down the side of her head onto her Under Armor workout shirt.

She winces, "Don't touch me. I think I have some broken ribs. Go call an ambulance."

I reach for my cell phone and dial 9-1-1, telling the voice what I found.

"Is there anyone else hurt?" the man asks.

I pause and my mouth gapes open, "I'm not sure, I haven't looked. However, I know for sure one person is."

"We will send an ambulance right away, hold on."

I release a sigh, "Will do. Bye."

As the line goes dead I stuff my phone into my back pocket and head towards the staircase. There are boot prints imprinted into the fancy and expensive carpet which is not a good sign. I groan and stoop down to look at them closer. They're definitely man shoe prints and there aren't any men in the Henderson's family that go down the stairs.

"Aw forget it! There better not be someone down here or else I will legit crap my pants. Like I am so serious RN, it's not even remotely funny. So be a gentleman— or woman because villains come in both sexes and I am not sexist—and state your presence," I gulp as my feet hit the bottom step. I flip on a light and to my surprise there isn't anyone there, but on the wall is a dagger which was stabbed into the drywall, a note attached to the hilt.

If you want her then she'll die.

I stare at the note, attempting to comprehend the saying. It made no sense at all. When I realize the meaning, and the subject of the note, the note falls to the floor as I run to Anna's room and throw her bedroom door open so hard it bangs against the wall.

"ANNA!" I scream. "ANNA!!! THIS IS NOT FUNNY! ANNA?"

Her bed isn't made, her comforter lays on the floor, which is not something my best friend would allow unless it was finals week, which it wasn't.

She was taken.

I collapse onto the floor and hold my head in my hands, trying not to cry. This is what Phantom and I were trying to avoid! How come it happened the minute I accepted Maine's challenge? Was she behind the threat to Anna? I muse on it for a moment and decide that there were two separate stories going on at once. My story and Anna's. Shame I don't know much of Anna's story. I dwell on the thought and come up with something small.

A young girl, terrible at school but a kick-butt superhero who is able to transform into any animal she wants, while fighting off her attraction for her nemesis/love interest. She has a target on her back but doesn't know it. Her best friend has become closed off, and worries about everything and she doesn't know why. She just lives her everyday life, and tries not to focus on the obvious fear in her friend's eyes.

I am the worst person on this planet.

I pull out my cell phone and dial Anna's number. It could be a giant risk, but I needed to know if she wasn't just going into town even though her car was parked in the driveway.

The line goes dead within a few rings. No answer or no voicemail.

Tears start to stream down my face, and I punch the floor. Why? The second I put down my guard to see Maine, Anna gets taken!

Shakily, I get to my feet and walk to my room, sliding the closet doors open and pulling out a skull and crossbones tee and a black maxi skirt with my boots. I feel my hair shorten as I become Chaos and shed Kelsey.

I hear the sirens stop outside the house as I push open the window and scale the fire escape ladder. They'll find the front door smashed to pieces and immediately go inside. I hesitate for a moment before walking off the property and into the street. An EMT notices me and calls out.

"There's a woman unconscious in the kitchen, and a not downstairs on the basement floor. Kelsey Jerrs was not behind this, although it seems to me that she freaked out and left. It's unclear which villain did this, but Maine should be the first suspect, along with the freaking Brotherhood. I'm going to chat to Phantom for a moment, GTG," I wave and become invisible.

I have to make my steps lighter so my boots stop thudding against the pavement but I keep my fast pace. I soar through a kid on a tricycle, and he begins to cry after feeling my presence slid through his. His mother huffs and stands from the camping chair she was sitting in on the driveway. I can hear her trying to console the poor kid but have no time to apologize.

"Anna," I puff, my arms swinging against my sided as I run as fast as I can. I get to the edge of the neighborhood before stopping to catch my breath. It irks me that I am not in the best of shape, so I try to hover and fail immensely at that.

Should have driven... I think with an imaginary wail of dismay. Where am I even going?

But I know where I am going— I just don't want to admit it. Phantom's lair. Maybe it would be impossible to find, but I was going to try.

I hold my breath and someone walks right past me in the sidewalk. When the man gets far enough away, I let out a whoosh of air and begin walking towards the abandoned warehouses. This whole scenario began in a freaking warehouse so it could be my best option to begin there.

It takes a while, the sun beginning to set and all, until I get to the end of town. My phone is buzzing, Mr. Henderson's number flashing on the screen. He doesn't leave me any messages though, so I assume it's about the condition his wife is in or something. Every five minutes it would buzz and I would ignore it. One would think the calls would stop after ten tries, but alas it does not.

My stomach growls and I clench my middle. Bringing food would have been a good idea. In fact, bringing my Chaos backpack would have made my life so simpler. I packed it specifically for evenings like this. Go figure I'd forget it when I actually need it.

I trudge forward, to get a view in one of the basement windows. I know Phantom wouldn't be so stupid to have a window give away his hiding space, but I remember the black linoleum floors and there was a small chance that the entire warehouse had the same floors. The one that I peered into has fake marble tiles. Not a match.

With a sigh, I get back up and walk to the neighboring warehouse. That one is full of crates, and a security guard shines a dim flashlight around the room where he sits in a beach chair.

Not the one. I take in a deep breath, and let it out very slowly in an attempt to sate my annoyance. This could take weeks, I realize. I set my mouth in a determined frown, willing to take that much time. Surely school would understand why I missed.

School... The thought has me filled with dread. I have to go back so I don't fall behind. Anna was taken, would whoever took her take me as well? Did I have a target on my back as well? Too many questions plague my mind.

I just have to find Phantom.

My boots thud against the concrete as I run to the next few warehouses. None had black floors. I keep searching the entire part of town, which is a few miles stocked with warehouses of different sizes. The moon rises high into the sky as I search through the night. Sleep is ignored, and my growling stomach eventually stops complaining.

When I get to the other side of the warehouses I sit on a curb and put my face in my hands, trying hard to reign in the oncoming tears that threaten to fall. My jaw clenches with determination. Anna calls my determination my fatal flaw. If I want something then I will go to any extent whatsoever to get it. There wasn't a chance I would give up finding Phantom's hideout.

"C'mon! Where can you're retarded lair be?" I huff to the empty street. All of the warehouses are dark now, and peering into the windows is useless. All there can be seen is utter darkness.

A long time ago, I stopped being invisible. There is only two sources of light over where I am anyways, the moon and a single street lamp at the far edge of the road, so it's not like anyone could see me.

I need to find him. Neither Anna or I could afford my failure. The though makes me stand and cross the street to abandoned buildings now. Most have smashed in windows, so I go though them and look at the floor. Tile. Not the right type of flooring now.

Some buildings have basements, and I sink farther into the darkness but those basements usually have carpet or a mosaic of tiny tiles. One doesn't need sight to tell that it's all wrong.

While checking out one building, I hear something run away from me and squeak. My blood freezes under my skin. Rats.

"Shoot," I whisper. Anything breathing that is smaller than me makes me completely terrified. I gulp and slowly head back up the stairs, not daring to touch the handrail. Something crunches under my boots and I figure it's got to be rat feces. The though makes me dry heave as I reach the main floor and run to the door.

My heart races in my chest as I check the bottom of my boots to have it be confirmed. My face goes deathly pale. The things I do for my best friend...

I stare at the offending building for a while until I see a curtain move just slightly in the second story window. My mind rushes to every single horror movie Mrs. Henderson has made me watch with her and I gulp. There is a chance that it was just a breeze even though the night is so still.

Or it could be–

Hands grab my waist roughly, "Boo!"

I scream bloody freaking murder and whip around to see him, wide smirk on his face.

"You know it's three fifteen in the morning, right? Why are you here of all places?" Phantom inquires tiredly.

"Anna got kidnaped," I gasp, still thoroughly out of breath.

His eyes narrow, "I heard about that. When I tried to look for you, your father asked me if I had seen a girl named Kelsey and that she ran from the scene. He was very pissed off by the way and worried about you. Oh wait, he wasn't pissed off, I was royally pissed off. Still am BTW. Why didn't you, oh IDK, stay the frick where you were? Eh? Any response for that? Maybe I'm still too pissed to hear the answer. All I know is that I'm going to kill you and enjoy every moment of it."

Dread pools in my lower stomach, "Please don't kill me."

His green eyes are full of evil intentions as we lock gazes. He digs his fingers into my hair and grips it tightly, "I'm really upset at you. Why are you so difficult? I want to keep you safe! That's all I want!"

Phantom forces my head back so my neck is exposed. I hold my breath as his lips attack my neck, biting my flesh. Heat creeps up to my cheeks as he tugs my hair.

My hands come up to push him away but he doesn't budge.

"Phantom!" I yell, shoving him hard. He steps back, that smirk pasted on his face as his eyes scan my neck appreciatively.

"Are you a vampire or something?" I gasp, looking at him incredulously. My hair is a mess and I try to flatten it down.

"If I'm sparkling Edward, does that make you gloomy Bella?" he retorts with a snort.

I glare at him.

"Well since it's three in the morning and we both haven't slept and I hate dealing with cops... let's go to my lair," he suggests.

I give him a disgusted look, "That's what I was looking for! But since you attacked me and am upset with me I don't think I'm going with you!"

"Babe, I'm not upset, I'm pissed."

"Makes me want to go with you even less..." I mutter.

"I have a car," he bribes.

I admit, when he said the word car my eyes met his for a moment before flashing back to the ground.

"You can come with me or I could drape your body over my shoulder and make you come. You know how much I love to do that."

I deliberate for a moment, "Okay. I'll come."

Chapter 21

I wake up with a slight headache on the cold, hard floor. Sitting up, a groan escapes my lips and I wonder where the heck I am until I see Phantom sitting in a black couch. His shoes are kicked off and he took off his suit coat and unbuttoned the top buttons of his shirt. It's the most disheveled I have ever seen him, even with the one time where Apeman threw him into the sewer full of caca. Thinking about it makes me laugh and Phantom just shakes his head at me.

"I've always known that you are insane, but how insane I have yet to figure," he mutters under his breath but loud enough for me to hear.

I try to stand up only for the world to tilt on its axis so I sit back down and groan, "What the flapjacks did you do to me?"

"If crazy equals genius..." Phantom sighs and stands up. "I used the forget me stick. Ever seen Megamind?"

I rub my forehead, "It hurts! Did you really KO me with a stick? Here I was thinking that you did have some decency to you after all..."

"I could be indecent if you would like me to be. Just say the words 'Phantom, strip' and I will do it."

I look at him like he was moldy cheese, "Uh, N to the O thanks. I think I'd rather skinny dip in the sewer lines like the one time Apeman threw you-"

His gloved hand covers my mouth and he looks pissed off, "While I would very much love the chance of seeing you skinny dip in any pool or sewage line, I would advise you to shut up."

There is silence and he slowly takes away his hand, giving me a weary glare. "We need to find Anigirl sooner rather than later. That increases the chance that she's still breathing significantly if we find her within twelve hours. I have Rush sniffing around for her scent or any dang trace of her but so far he has combed Main Street down to Thirty-Second Avenue without a single wiff of her presence. You know Anigirl the best so can you think of any place she would go if she wasn't kidnaped? Any safe havens?"

I nod, "She would go to her friend's house. There are two boys named Ryan and Luis but she rarely hangs out with them after school-"

"We'll start with them. Do you know where they live?" he cuts me off.

"Yeah, from my house..." I say but in reality I only have a slight idea of where Luis lived.

"Well that works out because your Dad thinks that Kelsey has also been kidnapped. Why don't you go home and we'll start from there?"

I look around the room, "This is not your lair. I spent all night looking for it and you didn't even take me there."

"You're right, but I thought that you were too familiar of the place so I had to mess with you a bit. I admit, when you didn't bring it up before I believed that you didn't know the difference of my lair and... this place. You have officially fooled me for once in our lives."

"How many lairs do you have?" I ask in awe. Same color scheme of black and silver with hints of white but decorated differently with fewer screens of the city on the wall.

"I don't have to answer that but pick a number and multiply that by six."

I glare at him, "Another Megamind reference? Please tell me that you want to come to the light side of the force."

He pauses to think about it for a moment before returning those cold eyes to mine, "Not a chance in hell."

"That's where you'll go when you die if you don't stop being evil," I fire back.

He smirks, "You're interesting you know."

My head pounds and I squeeze my eyes close, "Ugh you totally suck Capri Suns! Why'd you hit me in the head?"

"Don't be a crybaby."

I open my eyes to stare at him for a moment, "Was that a Melanie Martinez reference?"

"Who?" he asks innocently

I shake my head, "You're confusing me and my head hurts already. How many references can you make?"

An evil laugh escapes his lips, "Well you could set yourself on fire but you're never gonna learn."

I try to stand up again and fall over, "I can't even stand! How hard did you hit me? We can't do anything if I'm like this! We need to find Anna! Don't you know who took her?"

"I looked at the note and I do have a list of acquaintances that like to leave love letters. It's a long list though, and only a few of them are on the grid."

I sigh, "You're absolutely useless."

Phantom's jaw almost drops to the ground, "Useless? Excuse me but when have I ever been useless?!"

I laughed and crawled over to the couch, lifting myself to lay down on it, "You aren't really useless. I'm just annoyed."

He walks over to me, "Well then let's get going. Maybe that will lift your spirits." Phantom reaches on the coffee table and hands me a mug, "Drink up."

The mug's contents look like mud, "Uhhh I don't think so..."

Phantom gives an exasperated huff before taking the mug and taking a swig. I notice that he doesn't swallow as he looks at me and then pulls my face to his. The liquid enters my mouth and I gag but swallow it. The drink doesn't taste bad but the fact that it's from Phantom's mouth gets me hot and flustered and makes me want to puke at the same time. Almost instantly, the pounding in my skull stops.

He pulls away and my mouth is still open, "Oh."

"Oh is right. Drink up or do we need a repeat?" he raises an eyebrow.

I take the cup, "I'm good! I'll drink it!"

"Good Chaos. Hurry up as we don't have all day."

I chug the drink super fast and then stood up, "Let's go! Anna needs us!"

He leads me out of the room and up the stairs.

"Is this a house?" I wonder as the open foyer to the front door.

"Of sorts," he replied vaguely.

"So it's kind of a house?" I poked his back. "How is that even possible?"

"This place is just a skeleton of what it once was. It's missing some key elements though that make it a home one could say."

I think about what he has just said for a few minutes as a silver sports car with a low growling engine pulls up. The driver gets out of the car, tips his hat to Phantom, "Mr. Rhodes."

"Phantom right now, Richard," Phantom reminds icily. I rack my brain, Mr. Rhodes was Phantom's real last name? Did I know him? I think about it for a moment and Phantom whacks me in the face with a gloved hand, "I can see the hamster wheel spinning and I don't like it. The probability of you having ever heard of me before is close to none so don't think too hard about it."

I smirk at the venom in his voice, "You know who I am so it's fair that—don't say that life's never fair so suck it up either, that is so lame sauce I swear!—I get to know who you really are."

His lips pouted, "Nah, that would spoil the fun!" Silence breaks as we sit in the car and the driver clicked a touch screen with 'Kelsey Jerrs Home' button on it. I narrow my eyes at the button as the route turns up to the Henderson's home. I always knew Phantom was a stalker type of guy, but this was completely on a whole other level.

The engine of the car starts and I just want to bury myself in a hole with the thick silence between us.

Eventually Phantom pokes me in the gut, "Penny for your thoughts?"

I glare at him, "I would like to know what you are thinking right now."

He just smirks at me and doesn't answer anything. It's frustrating but I know that I can't push him or else he'll close up on me completely.

Then I realize that I had given him a piece of my thoughts. I face palm and glare at him hard enough to to make my forehead hurt with the creases. "You conniving little loser. I really hate you right now," I tell him.

He smiles evilly at me, "This round's winner is me sweetie pie."

Chapter 22

When we pull up to the Henderson's home, I get out of the car before the driver can put the gears into park. There are remnants of caution tape by the door, but I kick it out of my way, entering into the dark house. The sun begins to rise as early morning approaches and I feel dread knot up in my stomach as I think about what Anna must be going through. I try not to ponder on that too much though.

I feel Phantom put a hand on my shoulder and I tense for a moment. He doesn't release me, but his hand gently guides me to the kitchen, all around the main floor of the mansion before we head first up the stairs to the master suite. The whole time I look for anything I might have missed during the initial scene, Phantom's guiding hand doesn't leave. I feel comforted by that fact, although I know I should stay on guard around my nemesis. I stop to take in the unmade, king sized bed. In the few years that I lived under the Henderson home, I have never once seen that bed not made. My feet were planted in the carpet as I stared at the gold sheets, and the used pillows in alarm.

Sensing my panic, Phantom nudges me out of the room, "Anigirl's father slept here last night I believe."

"What about her mom? She always makes the bed. Sometimes, I swear she does it in her sleep. Mrs. Henderson makes the bed so much that I never knew the sheets were friggin' gold silk. That's cliche as crap. Silk sheets..."

"Not a fan of silk?" Phantom inquires as we head down to the basement.

"Not particularly. I mean, there are better ways to blow money than buying sheets," I explain.

"But having sex in scratchy cotton sheets is so awkward. Trust me, once you go silk you will never turn back," Phantom stated.

I glare at him as we go down into the basement, "I thought you are a virgin?"

He glares at me, "I never said either or. Whichever one makes me more villainy and turns you on. Those are the only things I care about."

It is useless to respond, so I ignore him. I tap a fingernail against the wall by a hole where the note was, "I found a note here that said Anna was taken. It was a calling card I assume, but I have never seen one so plain. Usually people like you like to sign your work."

"Every villain who is actually a villain leaves some kind of signature. You just have to find it. Sometimes it is very obscure, and other times it is plain as day, but unless it's a wannabe, there always is some kind of signature."

I raise an eyebrow, "You don't have a signature."

He smirks, "Of course I do. I'm not someone who declares himself a villain for no reason now am I? Think about all my crimes. How do I like to kill?"

He likes to rip out people's organs... I think to myself.

His eyes narrow as Phantom studies my face to see if I get what he said. Satisfied, he turns to the door of my room, "I love being down here. It's so warm and it smells like your lotion. Mmmmm..."

I flick on the light as he just lets himself in my room, "It's not like you haven't been here before so I don't get the whole excitement you have about my room."

Phantom walks around slowly, his eyes drinking in every little trinket that I own. I stand in the doorway and just watch him do his thing curiously. His eyes are narrow in thought and there is a crease in his forehead as he tries to link things to a signature.

A few minutes later he sighs and looks me in the eye, "Nothing. Let's try Anna's room and then the rest of the basement before going upstairs and checking out the whole house."

"I could have told you there wasn't anything in here," I roll my eyes.

"But you didn't. I think you like me in your room, so you kept your mouth sealed," Phantom retorts.

I swallow as my cheeks turn pink and I scurry to Anna's room. the first thing I notice is that her quilt is on the floor. The bed sheets are all unnaturally rumpled like someone took her out of her bed and she tried to fight back.

"She was taken from her bed," I say to Phantom, pointing at the bed. Something crunches under my foot and I look down to see a bottle of her Daisy Perfume shattered on the ground, the liquid already seeped into the carpet.

"When she sees her favorite bottle of perfume smashed, Anna's gonna get P-I-double S-E-D..." I mutter to myself.

"Looks like she fought back, which could have ruined the signature... or maybe not," Phantom replies as he looks at a One Direction poster with red lipstick all over it. I gasp for two reasons. One, that poster was from Anna's first One Direction Concert and it was majorly special to her, and two, the scribbles made Phantom's unnaturally pale complexion turn even paler the longer his eyes looked at it. But Phantom must have been frozen in place because he doesn't move an inch. His wide eyes just drink in the red lipstick until I forcefully grab his arm and turn him towards me.

"What the heck is that scribble?" I demand, slapping both of my palms on his cheeks to pull him out of his shock. "I know that it's not Maine's doing. She leaves me music and apple pie. Darn apple pies..."

"You are not going to school for a while. You aren't going to leave my side for forever. You aren't allowed to even pee without me anymore. Shoot..." he whispers so lowly I could barely make it out.

I swallow loudly, "Umm, I thought you were the worse villain out there so who makes you scared? Not that I don't like to see you scared, it's just the thought of you being scared of anything makes me want to cry and hide in the Appalachian Mountains..."

"It's wintertime, the Appalachian Mountains are covered in snow so we can't hide you there. I know my family has a villa in Greece. Want to go to Greece for a while?" Phantom responds.

"While Greece sounds exotic, I would really like to get Anna back from whoever took her so I know she's alive."

"Had to try," he sighs again and runs a hand through his hair.

"That mark is from the leader of the Brotherhood. You might know of him, although he 'retired' when we were in Junior High. But he still leads the Brotherhood and he still commits crimes here and there. I've worked with him before and he is so amazingly good at what he does it's uncanny. It's been a few years since I've seen him though, and last I heard he was in Russia taking out some mobsters that thought they were too good for the mob anymore. Or was it Ireland...?" he trails off deep in thought.

"What's his name Phantom? I can Google the rest so you don't end up having a freaking panic attack."

"The best way to stop me from having a panic attack is for you to kiss me," he replies.

"For the love of everything awesome, just tell me."

"He goes by the name of The Doctor," he grits through his teeth.

That sparks something in my memory, "Maine had an affair with him when I was little."

Phantom looks at me with an unreadable expression, "What?!"

"Yeah,he came over a few times. I remember because he always cut Maine while they were kissing but she liked it... and that sounds SO gross so I'm gonna stop."

A string of swearwords left his lips, "Are you for real? That totally makes sense to me. That little bugger... I swear I'm going to kill him and stuff his liver into his wife's pillow so she can sleep on it."

"Let's go to my summer home in California. It's nice weather over there, and the ocean is magnificent. I think you'll like it there," Phantom states abruptly.

"Not until we get Anna back. If The Doctor is as scary as you're acting then we need to get Rush and I know of a few heroes that could probably help me out," I suggest.

Phantom laughs but it doesn't have an ounce of humor in it, "Sweetie, you're gonna need a whole army of heroes to take him out."

It was my turn to curse, "Really?"

"I am not even exaggerating a little bit. There's a reason why he isn't locked up or that a hero didn't kill him. It's damn near impossible to do either."

"Then we're going to die. I'm okay with that fact, are you?" I ask.

He looks me in the eye for a moment, "As long as it's by your side I wouldn't mind anything."

For a moment my heart gets all warm and fuzzy and then the smell of apples wafts down to my nose and I scream bloody murder.

Chapter 23

It is reflex, the urge to cover my nose and throw up at the scent of apples baking in the oven. I hold a hand over my nose and swallow hard, looking at Phantom with wide, scared eyes. I know what the pie would look like once I see it. The lattice crust, and the never dents that circled the pie full of gooey apples and cinnamon glaze. It would be perfect if I go upstairs right away, because Maine never left me an underdone or overdone pie before. I don't know how she makes the scent so infiltrating in one's home if she bakes her pies off site.

"Speaking of signatures..." I mumble, crossing my arms over my chest.

"Maine is here, isn't she?" Phantom asks, but it doesn't seem like I need to answer so I don't even give him a nod.

"I hate, hate, hate apple pie!" I yell to nobody in particular. The basement echoes my scream as I turn to stomp up the stairs

"Nobody said you had to like it," Phantom retorts as he follows me up the stairs. "Calm down a bit."

"Calm down?" I laugh humorlessly, "How the crap can I calm down when she's here?"

"You fight her. Simple enough," Phantom stops on the stairs to shrug and look at me.

I give him a deep glare as the idea seems so crazy, "How can I fight her when you don't think I'm strong enough? We've only trained once, and I know that you think my punches suck Capri Suns."

The edges of his lips twitch as he forces not to smile at my reaction, "But I'm with you so you should be fine... I believe."

I scoff, "That's totally reassuring. I feel so calm right now as I walk up the stairs to my eminent death. Thank you so much, Phantom."

"Anymore of that sass and you'll be stressing words like I do," he responds.

"You have the strangest of speech patterns. It's not norm al... maybe you need to get that checked out."

He smirks at me, and then takes my arm to drag me towards the kitchen. I am dragged towards the oven, where a perfect apple pie is baking, the top already a gorgeous light brown color. The smell makes me want to gag, so I hold my breath and breathe only when I have to.

I hear high heels clack against the tile and I stiffen, looking in the direction of that blasted noise I know will bring in the last person I ever want to see again.

Maine walks in, her fiery red hair resembling a tumbleweed since she never brushes it. I gulp, and Phantom looks from her to me and back to Maine. She smiles warmly at me, and I can see the crazed look in her eyes. The padded cell and psychotic treatments didn't do her any good. She's the same as she always is, just full of more rage.

Something cold presses underneath the back of my shirt and I start. Phantom hands me my silver gun, and I wonder how he got that. I reach behind me and take it so that Maine doesn't see what I have.

"My dearest Kelsey. Have you figured out which game we are playing? I know you have, so why don't you tell--"

"YOU TOOK ANNA! GIVE HER BACK TO ME!" I scream on the top of my lungs, cutting Maine's speech short.

Maine glares at me, lips turing into a pout. She despises when I interrupt her, which is part of the reason why I did so. "I didn't take your BFF," she sniffs.

"You had someone else do it for you! Does The Doctor mean anything to you?" Phantom asks.

"A man with a blue box?" Maine asks innocently. She opens the oven door and pulls out the pie without using oven mitts. I know her skin is burning off, yet I also know that she likes the pain. A part of me is concerned and another part of me is repulsed by the lack of self-preservation she has.

The woman eyes me as she sets her creation down on the counter and she doesn't look away as I meet her gaze evenly.

I look away first, since she is the one who gave birth to me... even though she got angry when I tried to take my own life and failed. She screamed that if I wanted to do so, then I should succeed so she doesn't have to feed me anymore.

Ah, childhood. How did I not become a villain?

"You have been messing around with The Doctor and you know it. He's the one who took Anna," Phantom explains, his voice unnaturally calm.

"And you would know, being his son and all, Colton," Maine pointed out, tilting her head back and laughing at him.

Colton.

That's Phantom's name?!

Colton Rhodes.

My jaw dropped onto the ground. The Rhodes Family!!! They were the richest people in the town! The father, Marshall Rhodes was a Senator, and his wife Sierra was a model. They had... five boys.

There were five boys that made up the Brothers originally, before they branched to become the Brotherhood. Sometimes, people still refer to the original group as the Brothers.

The Rhodes were the villains. They were the masterminds behind all the crimes in America—if not the world.

Phantom looked at me, with an evil smirk, "Cat's out of the bag now. Don't make too many assumptions, Kelsey. They won't be too true."

"That's right, because the Cardinales took you under their wings. He's like a servant for them," Maine interjected.

The Cardinales? How did they fit into this equation?

Phantom saw my confusion, "My mother is a Cardinale. The father's sister. The Brotherhood is made up of all the males of both families. We like to think of it like a mob family. I am definitely no servant," he scoffs the last part out and eyes me carefully.

"If it makes you feel any better I don't know who Rush is," Maine chimes. I glare at her. That does not make anything better for me! I know his identity! I should send both of their butts in jail!

But when push comes to shove I know that I will never really be able to lock up Phantom's sexy beast in jail. That would mean that I have won and my life would go back to what it was the short few days of my superhero life when I didn't know of Phantom and he kept track of me via the news before engaging me head on. That wasn't fun at all. I had to go searching for trouble or trouble would search for me and I would never know who's hit list I was on, which meant I wasn't properly prepared for the battles, and Anna had to save my rear end most of the time.

Maybe my early days were the reason that my popularity is so low? I frown at the thought before turning to Maine, "The police know your secret identity, so they should be tracking you right now. This house is full of cameras— can't have priceless pieces of art and precious artifacts stolen from a mansion now can we?"

Phantom knows I am exaggerating a bit. Sure the Henderson home had cameras, but the kitchen doesn't so there aren't any here... and the more I think about the layout of the security system, the more I gather that it is completely possible for Maine to enter in this house unnoticed. I begin to worry as I know that Maine chose this room for the oven, but does she also know that there aren't any surveillance here? My palms clench into fists.

"Let them come join the party. I'll just kill them. I like to kill men in handsome uniform. Make the blue all stained with red. It's my favorite color, the red," Maine's gaze glosses over and I know that she is picturing it all. I blink back my disgust and Phantom laughs like the maniac that he is.

"I like their not-so manly screams," he states to Maine.

"Well I like it when the police are alive, thank you. You two are both psycho and need a straitjacket that is impossible for either one of you to get out of. How was the loony bin Maine? Did you like your soft padded cell? I hoped it was cozy, I mean I am your daughter so I made sure to get the softest padding and the most annoying doctors to keep you company."

Her eye twitches and I know that I have won this round. It's all true, I made sure to get the doctors that were able to check on her every hour on the hour because I know how much Maine hates repetition, and I especially know that she hates order. So the doctors kept her on a tight schedule.

"I told one doc that my own daughter sent me here. You know what he did? He looked at me and asked if I really did have a daughter that wasn't as screwed up as I was. I know my Kelsey is Chaos, which means you are effed for sure. You like violence, you like being able to use your mind to save the day. You love the challenge of being a hero, and you take immense pride that someone like Colton could possibly want to fight with a nerd like you. Honey, you aren't really pretty, but you know that and Phantom just has to butter you up with his words and his kisses and you are putty in his gloved hands. All he wants is sex," she chimes.

I growl, "Shut up! I am nothing like you! I am not 'effed' as you so unceremoniously put it. Next year I can get into any Ivy League school I want, which is definitely not something you would be able to do!"

"Your father attended Notre Dame you know," Maine shares.

"Then I would like to think that my father was smart, even if he slept with a crazy old bat like you," I put as sharply as I could.

That makes her pause for a moment, and turn to pull out a knife from the magnetic strip hanging on the wall. Phantom tenses but I know what she's going to do and it isn't anything violent. Well, it could turn into violence if I play my cards wrong and piss her off, but I do not intend for that to happen.

She cuts the pie, and steam rises into the air where it then disperses. The scent of apple pie is even more evident and my eyes water with disgust. "Where are the plates?" she asks me innocently.

I point to the right cabinet door, "I do not want any, so don't cut a slice for me."

"Me either, Maine," Phantom adds. I look at him and he winks at me.

She pouts like I know she would. I click my teeth together before saying, "Nah, Phantom wants some, so cut him a slice. He's a boy and you know the way boys think with their stomachs."

"That's sexist," Phantom mutters, but cautiously accepts a slice. He doesn't touch it though, but he stares at it for a moment as Maine hands him a fork. I know what he's doing.

In his mind he is wondering if it is poisoned or not. I do the same thing, but Maine's pies never are. But I wasn't expecting Phantom to refuse, and by the set of Maine's mouth, I know she's bothered by it.

"Try it," Maine chimes. I know it's Phantom's one and only warning that if he doesn't then the knife is going to be thrown at his head faster than he could react.

I don't know how he is going to react, so I brace myself for the worse.

And Phantom doesn't pick up his fork.

Chapter 24

It is so instant. The way that Maine's eyes immediately flash with violence. Before I have time to react, she pushes the pie off the counter where the glass shattered into millions of little pieces. She jumps onto the counter with a blade in hand and slashed at Phantom. I gasp as I watch blood begin oozing out just above his collarbone but not quite at his neck, his dress shirt staining with crimson. Even though he is wounded, Phantom doesn't even take notice of the pain. Instead, he grabs the arm that held the knife and squeezed, forcing Maine's hand to open and the knife fall to the ground.

There was pure fury in Phantom's eyes as he looked at Maine, "I don't want your damn pie. Not because you made it but because we both know what is in it, and we know it isn't good. Don't get your panties in a twist and lash out because I didn't take a bite. Be a little smarter than that, Maine."

A shiver ran through me as Phantom's voice was icy and sharp. There was absolutely no more warmth that emanates from him, but rather a blizzard's cold. My eyes look from the two people as I try to take in everything that happened, "Maine! What did you put in the pie? You never put anything in the pie, so why would you do so now? Is this part of the game, that I cannot even trust you? What is you angle?" I ask.

She looks at me, her eyes still full of violence, "I put cumin in it."

There is silence for a moment as I try to process what she said, "Why the heck is that such a big deal?"

Maine looks at Colton expectedly, and he locks his jaw and unlocks it. "Cumin... is my... kryptonite..." he whispers so silently that I barely hear it.

Maine begins to cackle as I stare at Phantom for the longest time. "Are you effing kidding me?" I wonder, dumbfounded beyond belief. Phantom, number one on the hottest villain chart, is allergic to cumin. CUMIN.

"It's fatal," he responds quietly, and for the first time, I see Phantom look vulnerable and actually human. His eyes are not longer full of confidence but rather hold uncertainty in them. It's so odd for me to see. I can't take my eyes off of him, because I know that once I do, his facade will return and this moment is worthwhile. I have to keep staring at him for a moment more. My mind is calculating, and I know that the plate with a piece of pie is still in front of Phantom, by Maine's knees as she kneels on the countertop.

I reach for the plate, picking up the fork and taking a bite. The flavor makes me choke for a moment before I swallow it whole. There is no way I could chew something so utterly disgusting. It takes all my might to smile and claim, "Wow Maine! Your pie is so good!"

There is no way for me to expect her reaction. Once she gets violent, it is hard to control her. But I know that she is my mother, and I know her better than anyone else. The one person who could gamble with her is me.

Maine's eyes light up, and a creepy smile flashes across her face, "My baby girl ate my pie!"

I gulp as she steps down from the counter and her arms embrace me in a hug. My body stiffens, unused to the attention. I know for sure that Maine never hugs. Was that pie such a big deal to her? There's no way of knowing what is going on in that psychopath's head. She must have wanted some form of praise if she was willing to go far enough as to give me a hug in reciprocation.

Pulling away from her embrace, I fidget with the hem of my shirt, twisting the fabric around my fingers and releasing it. It comes back against my skin with a snap and it makes me flinch in pain.

Phantom snorts at me and Maine smiles evilly at me. I ignore both of them and walk around the counter to pick up the large pieces of glass that were nearby, tossing the many pieces into the trash bin. As I busy myself with cleaning up, I hear Phantom ask Maine, "So you're saying that Doctor has Anna?"

I look up at him briefly and then dump some more of the glass into the trash. A shard cuts my hand but it isn't bad enough to bleed so I don't worry about it. When I look up at Maine once again, I see her eyeing the door. She fidgets, feeling remorse for what she attempted to do to Phantom in a small way. That's Maine's weakness. Her remorse.

"Feel free to leave if you'd like. You just have to tell us where Anna is," I say smoothly as I can. My eyes narrow at her and I wait patiently, checking the cut to see a small bead of blood on my palm. I wipe it against my shirt nonchalantly but Phantom notices the action. Nothing goes past his eyes.

Maine takes a deep breathe and looks me in the eyes, "She's at his house. If you know Doctor's identity, then you know where he lives. She's there in the basement of course. Cold and alone. Maybe starving... I didn't really give him too many rules except for the fact he cannot cut her open in any way. She's you're friend, and this is the game. Play it very carefully."

Suddenly Rush appears and tackles Maine to the ground, "You are going to spend the rest of your life in Hell!" he yells, yanking Maine's arms behind her back and forcefully pulling her to stand.

Maine just laughs, I can tell that she was terrified of Rush and his big stature since she doesn't even try to resist his grip.

"Take her back to her cell and make sure she doesn't get out again. I want a change in everyone she comes in contact with on a daily basis- her shrinks, her doctors, hell, even her visitors. She is not escaping again," Phantom orders Rush.

Rush looks at me with his big brown eyes, "Find Anna quickly. Statistics show that if you don't find her in twenty-four hours, then the victim is usually dead."

I sink onto the floor in despair, "Twenty-four hours? I have no idea who the Doctor is unless he's Matt Smith! How am I supposed to find him?"

"He's the father of the Cardinales," Phantom whispers as Rush drags Maine out of the house.

I look at him in shock, "So we have to go to the Cardinale's house? There's so much security even I couldn't get in if I were invisible!"

"I could, you'd only have to trust me..." Phantom trails off, looking at me for my reaction.

My eyes meet his for a long moment, "What's your plan?"

"First, I have to change in a secure location. Can't saunter in looking like Phantom when Doctor is supposed to be at ease of my presence. I'm staking high claims that he doesn't know Rush and I love our nemesis behind his back. If he does then we're in deep trouble. This whole plan might as well fail miserably."

"Maine wouldn't tell him that you're working with me," I state, then bite my lip because I know how unpredictable Maine is and there was a possibility that she could have told the Doctor and betray Phantom and Rush. "How does she know that you're Colton?"

Phantom runs a hand through his hair and sighs, "She used to hang around a lot when I was young. I think they were partners for a few months. My mom got very jealous and thought that he was being unfaithful to his own wife and family. As far as I know, however, he never cheated."

"But somehow I was conceived," I state flippantly.

"I don't think Mr. Cardinale would ever want to sleep with Maine," Phantom pointed out.

"I'm pretty sure I have a dad somewhere on this planet," I huff.

"Let's focus all of our efforts on my plan. I will be right back, stay here. I know you have a hard time listening to me, but if you move out of this room then I will kill you."

"Don't worry, I'm sure there is cumin somewhere in a cabinet drawer..." I fire back.

Phantom frowns at me, then spins on his fancy heel of his fancy shoes and leaves.

As he leaves me alone, I sigh impatiently and park my rear on one of the bar stools, elbows on the countertop to hold my head. I feel the early effects of a headache and groan.

Operation Find Anna has taken off.

Chapter 25

I should have known trusting Phantom with Jorge was a stupid idea, yet I gave him the car keys anyways because I didn't fully thing it through until after he squealed the tires while getting out of the carport.

"He's sensitive!" I yell, petting the dashboard in front of the passenger's seat. "Go slower!"

Phantom doesn't was up on the gas, "We don't have a lot of time if you want Anna to be alive when we rescue her."

"Yeah, but if you do t be kind the Jorge then he will revolt and break down! Do you want to walk to wherever you're taking me to?" I retort.

"We wouldn't walk," he replies simply. I glare at him, though his eyes are focused on the road.

"You don't have your seatbelt on. That's my number one rule of people being in my car. You have to have a seatbelt," I chime.

He gives me a mean look. His signature mean look, "If we crash, I'll turn intangible and nothing will happen. What's the point of having powers if one does not care to use them?"

"Where are we going?" I ask impatiently as he turns on a dirt road.

He doesn't answer of course

Corn fields zoom past, and poor Jorge groans with the struggle of going off-road. I wince with every rock that bounces off my car. Even if they scratch, it would only add to the collection of dents. Phantom chuckles every time I grimace.

He's driving too fast to make conversation, the only sound is the road and rocks. I stare out at the sea of corn. It's almost harvest time, yet not quite. When he turns, I realize that I have no idea where we are going and the fact scares me. Phantom is a villain, and if we don't find Anna soon, then statistics prove that she'll be dead by the time I can reach her. I eye him and wonder if he's actually on my side.

The van slows to a stop and I look out to see a bare piece of the field.

"This is an A+ murder place..." I mumble, undoing the seatbelt.

"What a good idea! I'll remember that next time Detective Hawthorne decides to piss me off, or when my father decides to anger me by calling me and I need some people to kill to make myself feel better. Why go to therapy when you can take it out on other people?" Phantom turns to me with a cold smile.

It takes all of my willpower not to shiver, "If you kill anyone I'll put your butt in a jail cell faster than you can high tail it out of this forsaken town, Colton Rhodes."

Then something totally unexpected happens. Phantom puts the car in park and leans over to grab my chin and place his lips on mine.

I don't know how to react. It's so sudden! My heart beats super fast as his lips move against mine. My body leans towards him. His gloved hands stroke my cheeks, one moving to the back of my head. I seriously am in heaven, my arms locking around his neck, pulling him closer to me.

I think I moan. I know for sure he does. My face turns hot with a blush and I realize what I'm doing, what we are doing. I jolt back, dropping my arms, and putting enough distance as I possibly can in the van, which is more than a sports car would have. "Why?"

Phantom smirks, and motions to my neck. I look down to see the pendant necklace that stops a super's powers. My eyes widen, "What the heck Phantom?!" I yell.

"I love you and if you get in the Doctor's way, he'll kill you," he explains.

"You don't know that!" I fire back.

"I know a lot of things. For starters, there is absolutely no way that you can beat him when you barely defeat me on the insanely rare off-days I have."

"It wasn't ever my intention to kill you! I just put in you jail like I've done seventeen times before!" I raise my voice in defense.

"Was it seventeen? Seems It seems that I don't remember. But I do know that I've sent your sorry and plump rear end to a cell more than that..."

My cheeks are burning so much I know that I resemble a tomato. He only sent me to jail four times but his ego... To add to my embarrassment Phantom added as an after-thought, "Release your inner red-hot habanero fury upon me. There is still no way I'm taking you to the Brotherhood."

I grip the necklace. It was impossible for the wearer to remove it, yet I pulled it against my neck anyways, "How dare you do this! Anna is my best friend! You're going to let her die? I'll never forgive you!"

"I'll do anything to keep you alive, even if it means sacrific-ing someone else."

"What about Rush? He's in love with her you know! How are you going to look him in the eye- your best and possibly only friend- once you've killed his girlfriend?" I respond. There isn't any way that I am going to let him walk away from me. Wherever Phantom goes is where I am going. My mind is made up and I was set on it.

"I won't let you do that! She's my best friend! Why? Why are you like this?" I plead.

He points to himself, "Once a villain, always a villain."

"Well you know what? I hate villains!" I scream at him. It is totally unfair of me to say, but I am angry at him. All I want is for him to hurt as much as I am. It isn't right, but I trusted him. Yet here he is turning against me. I should have known he would do this.

"Hate and love are very similar. When a person feels those emotions they have to be very particular about which line they cross. I'm pretty sure we both have crossed the hate line to love," he says in an icy tone. A gloved hand reaches out to brush my hair away from my face.

I slap his hand away, "Take the pendant off of me right now."

"No can do, princess," he sighs, eyes drifting to my chest where the necklace rests.

I reach for the door handle, and get out of the car. It seems almost instantaneous that Phantom is behind me, his arms around my chest so I can't escape him. "Where do you think you're going?" he hisses in my ear. His teeth nip at my earlobe and I swallow hard, heart rate increasing dramatically.

"Where. Are. You. Going?" he repeats sterner than before when I don't answer.

"Anna needs me," I choke out as a gloved hand slides up and down one of my arms. "I refuse to leave her to die. I'm a hero and heroes save people."

"And villains kill heroes. Since you are too confident, let me enlighten you a bit before you do anything retarded. The doctor has quite the reputation. He's killed Bonder, Jettson, Undermire, Wirewrap, and Streech... to name the ones I know about. There are more less known heroes that he's taken care of as well. Nobody fully knows his powers. If you don't know what a man like him is capable of then how can you even plot against him? You'd have to be out of your mind."

"Good thing I'm crazy!" I interject, trying to shake him off. His hand won't stop rubbing against my arm, and my heart-beat won't slow down to a healthy pace. I can feel his entire body against mine and I fit into his build so well it seems perfect.

Phantom's lips press against the hollow of my throat, "Doctor is a maniac. He's killed five times more people than I have, and you know how bloody my hands are."

"Together we can take him down!" I try.

"No. We both cannot even take him down. We need more allies."

"We aren't doing anything productive right now, are we?" I spit.

"If you would just sit here and wait for me to talk to people, that would be nice. But instead here we are bickering away. Be reasonable," he sighs.

I shake my head, "You're going to get some other villains to take him down without me. It's a coup d'etat sort of thing. No way."

"Kelsey, if I have to I will chain you to Jorge's steering wheel and take the keys so you can't escape. Don't think for a second I won't."

"Screw you!" I yell, wiggling against him.

"Wouldn't you love to?" he asks me with a light groan.

I freeze, completely embarrassed, "That's not what I meant."

"Sure it is. Now let me go talk to people I know and then I'll be back. Easy peasy. You'd better suit up as Chaos. Wouldn't want these acquaintances to know your secret ID..." he tsked.

"Yeah, Colton," I growl.

He sighs with contentment, "I love it when you say my name. It sounds so sexy coming out of that mouth of yours. You know I've had dreams where you've screamed it so loud your voice goes "

I roll my eyes, "Let me go!"

To my surprise he did. I stepped away from him to get my bag out of the car. Next thing I know, I was collapsed against the front seat...

...My hand chained to the steering wheel and Phantom nowhere to be seen.

"JERK!" I scream.

Chapter 26

He was going to die. As I twist my wrist within the confines of my handcuffs, my anger only growing. I wiggled to get my phone out but who was I going to call?

I lean over so my hand connected to the steering wheel and tugged on the pendent angrily. It did nothing useful of course. The wearer could never take it off. Frustrated, I lean back in the chair and stare at the roof of my car. My mind is reeling with different ways to exact my revenge. The best scenario is if possible, I can get free and then chase after Phantom. Though the idea seemed great, it wasn't any good if I couldn't get free. That task was becoming impossible without my powers.

As I struggled with being tied to the steering wheel, my wrists began chafing. The sun came through the untainted windows and I felt like my skin was baking even though it was fall. The stalks of corn swayed with the breeze and I became jealous. Those stalks were free while someone so lovingly tied my to my car! I growl with frustration and slump comfortably in the seat, settling to wait for his return and plotting his death.

I don't know how long I waited, baking in the sun. What I do know is that with every passing minute my anger was growing hotter and hotter.

I hear rustling among the corn and turn to face the direction. Sure enough, it isn't Phantom that shows but rather Rush's football build that appear. I narrow my eyes as he saunters to the driver's door and opens it, "Interesting."

"Interesting? Just get the pendant off of me!" I snap.

"Feisty. Who the crap pissed in your Cheerios?" he asks, a finger teasingly wrapping around the power-inhibiting necklace.

"Take a pick!" I huff.

"My cousin perhaps?" he guesses with a smile tugging on his lips.

"My best friend was taken and you were supposed to keep watch over her. What the heck happened? How could Anna have been taken when you're always around her?" I spit.

Rush frowns at me and taps his forefinger in the middle of my sweaty forehead, "You're temper is as blazing as this heat. Careful, I could just walk away and tell Phantom that you disappeared somehow. I lie all the time to him so he won't know any better."

"Get me out of here, and let's find Anna."

"Okay, okay," he relents, lifting the necklace off from around my neck.

"Halle-freaking-lleuiah," I sigh, hopping out of the car and standing on the fresh farmland dirt.

"For the record, you're anger cannot even hold a candle to how I've seen Phantom when he's upset. Usually you're doing, not to pin the blame on or anything."

I choose not to respond, but smirk. I know exactly what he is talking about. Or at least one instance.

It was when I was starting to shadow Anigirl. Back then, I wasn't sure if I like being a hero or anything but I loved the mind wars Phantom and I had. It was as addicting as heroine. I loved every moment that he worked my brain and called me out when I didn't reply fast enough. It was complete heaven in my eyes.

On that particular night, it was raining pretty hard and Phantom had decided to steal this top secret machine that makes rain turn to football sized hail. Don't ask me who the crap invented such a machine, and how he heard about it, but it ultimately ended up in the evil gloves of Phantom.

There were a lot of things that happened. The usual lame banter since I didn't quite have my arsenal of comebacks then. I didn't know how to control my powers then either. Anna was teaching me a few martial arts techniques but it wasn't a lot for me to use.

"Yo, Noob. Boob. Moo. Poo. Sue. Loo-"

"Shut up!" I cut Phantom off, running my hand through my soaked platinum hair.

"You're upset. Is it because I said boob?" he asked innocently. "Don't worry, you don't really have a rack so it shouldn't offend you any."

My hands balled into two tight fists. I knew that I had sufficient cleavage- more than Anna at least, "I might not be a

D-cup but you know what?" I countered as I walked towards him.

I could see the smirk on his face, liking the fact that I challenged him, "What noob?"

My combat boot connected with the one spot nobody should ever kick a boy.

He was livid. So livid that his face turned red with anger and he ended up destroying the machine and going home.

"And the name's Chaos, you jerk!" I called after he was gone for a few seconds.

So worth it. Even still.

"You mean when I kicked him where a man should never be kicked?" I ask Rush innocently.

"To name one instance," he admits, running a hand through his locks.

We start to walk deeper into the field. It was the way that Phantom left me, so I hope that we were going to meet up with him soon. I wonder what Phantom was planning anyways, ditching me like he did. Rush twirled the necklace around his hand and then unwrapped it. The motion is quite distracting as the gold chain glinted from the sunlight into my eyes. I squint and move a step behind Rush to avoid getting blinded.

He doesn't speak to me as we trek through the field. Stalks whip my arms as I try to make a pathway since Rush wasn't being a gentleman and helping me out. Red streaks adorned my forearms but I just remind myself that everything I am doing is for Anna. We need to save her before she is killed.

Killed. I flinch at the word. What would happen if she died? How would I handle it?

This silence is deafening! I think to myself before opening my mouth to break it, "Do you think she's alive?" I ask.

"Most likely," Rush answers. I frown at him. He could have lied and told me yes, but instead replies with most likely.

"Is Doctor ruthless?" I ask timidly.

"There is a good chance that Anigirl may be in physical pain. They don't call him Doctor for nothing."

I want to pull my hair out at his responses. Instead of asking another question I mutter, "I should have been taken. I'm tougher physically and mentally."

"Doctor probably knows that fact. He chooses his patients meticulously," Rush answers.

"You are not making me feel any better!" I exclaim, throwing my hand in the air.

"You should become Chaos right now," Rush suggests.

I stop in my tracks, "Fine. Give me a second then."

And as soon as I am done transforming, I see the reason why.

People. Lots of people. Lots of spandex too and capes.

Heroes and villains are all gathered. And leading them is Phantom.

Chapter 27

I was gonna cumin Phantom's eyeballs out when I get the chance to attack and get my hands on that spice. If I were a cartoon character, there would be fire blowing out of my ears. It is insane how many villains stood before me, some tatted up from the head down, some inhuman, some looking like business people, and others dressed so scandalously they could get locked up for indecency.

And in the front are the Brotherhood.

It was hard to swallow.

One villain of the Brotherhood has his hands on the shoulder of a young girl. Fern. My eyes widen at the sight and I can't believe that she would be somewhere like here. My eyes slide to Phantom and his trademark smirk is plastered on his face. All-knowing scumbag...

I point a finger at Fern, "You don't look like a villain to me. Why the crapola are you here?" Why you and not the evil villain Tera? I added in my mind. I mean, if we're talking about schoolmates that can totes be evil, she'd make numero uno and Fern would be dead last. She was FERN for crying' out loud! Geeky brown hair cropped short, green eyes, and thick glasses that took up her whole entire face.

"Let's get Anigirl," Rush roars to the crowd. There is silence and confused glances.

"Why in Hell would we save a hero?" one villain spoke up.

Phantom's smirk only widens into an evil smile, his green eyes lighting up, "We aren't here to save a stupid girl. Our mission is to take out the Doctor."

"No wonder you've called for an army," a girl yells in the back. She is dressed in furs and I wonder where she came from. Somewhere cold judging from the beads of sweat forming by her temple and running down the side of her face.

"It's an impossible task!"

I gulp, taking in the wide eyes and the shaking heads. Is it impossible to take out the Doctor? My palms clench into fists at my sides. He has Anna.

"What makes you think that Chaos will even help us in the act? She's a hero and a bad one at that. I bet she can't even beat Rush if she tried," a voice scoffs.

My eyebrows knit together. That voice is right. I can never defeat anyone except the stupid villains. Apeman bangs against his chest and glares at me. It is obvious I have talent, but what use is it when I cannot use that talent properly. It was like being able to read music yet having no idea how to play an instrument. Completely wasteful.

Fern walks up to me and takes my hand, "Steele, I think we should help her get her friend back and at least weaken this Doctor guy so that a few of us can have the chance to attack and take him out. Sounds like if you guys don't want to, you're all scaredy cats."

Her eyes bore into mine through the thick lens of her glasses and I can see that she knows something she isn't supposed to know. I blink a few times and look at the guy she was standing by.

"I've always wanted to usurp my father. Hay, how will your fiancee react when she finds out what we are up to?" Steele asked his brother.

Hayden Cardinale is dating Miss Benson. Are they engaged? I ponder on this for a moment before hearing his response, "She won't like it but if it's to save someone then she might appreciate it a little bit more. At least, I think..." his lips twist into a frown.

I look at Phantom, "Is everyone from your family here?"

He nods, "Not my mother or her aunt though. They're looking for his hideout. Any moment I should be getting a text that-" he paused and pulled out a sleek black phone.

"He's at Ridgeway!" Phantom's eyes light up with excitement and determination. "Anyone who would like to come can. I'm definitely not making you, but just know that it will be the talk of the century. What we do today may possibly change the world. How cool would that be? History created by villains."

"It could inspire other acts of villains against villains," Rush murmurs.

"A larger fighting pool!" a ninja looking guy thrusts his fist in the air elatedly.

There is some talking amongst the crowd and Phantom turns to me, "Let's go. Whoever want to come will follow. We cannot afford to wait any longer. Anigirl cannot afford us to wait any longer."

Rush runs a hand through his long hair, "There's a higher possibility that she's dead now. Statistics are not on our side anymore."

A pang of hurt runs through my entire body. Anna could be dead now. What if she was? What would I do? My throat constricts so much I cannot breathe. Tears well up in my eyes but I try to blink them back, gasping for air at the same time. This cannot be happening right now. I need to focus on Anna!

Phantom pulls me towards his chest and he melts into the ground. Once alone he picks me up and strokes my hair, "Don't freak out. Doctor likes to play around and mess with minds just as much as Maine does. There could be a chance that she is still alive. Hold onto that hope and let us save her."

Once I collect myself, I push away from his chest, turning intangible myself and begin to walk faster. Phantom leads me and we begin running as fast as we can. I can't help but wonder if it would be better to take Jorge, then remember villains are supposed to be following us.

"How do they know where to go?" I ask Phantom.

"Everyone else is following Rush who is following our vibrations in the ground. We villains have already set up a system."

I bite my cheek. Could I trust villains to help me? I know my influence in the hero community was embarrassingly weak, but villains have a higher chance of turning into traitors. I pray that nothing in the plan would go wrong and that Anna was alive. That hope is the only thing I can cling to.

"What is she is dead?" I whisper.

Phantom looks at me, "She shouldn't be."

I am not as sure. We slow down, and Phantom points up, "There's Ridgeway. According to Rush and a few others, Anna and Doctor are definitely in there. What do you want us to do?"

"I want to storm the building but that would be suicide. Are there any guards?"

Phantom shrugs his shoulder, "Rush didn't say anything about guards."

I hear an explosion and wince and the ground shakes, "I guess we are storming the place. Let's go."

"Your wish is my command."

We begin to climb up and when we reach the surface there is only one word to describe everything going on.

Pure. Utter.

Chaos.

Chapter 28

It is an experience, working with heroes and villains. One would say that sometimes joining forces in order to wipe out a common enemy for the greater good would be like it happens in the movies: everyone somehow reads each other's minds, knowing exactly what villains the hero needs to team up with to have the best combo attacks.

It doesn't work like that at all. In fact, I think the chaos of the situation made it a million times harder for me to take out the Doctor. Villains were fighting each other, and the few heroes rounded up were trying to pull the villains off one another, only getting into the crossfire themselves. There were people dressed in orange prison jumpsuits that were the Doctor's pawns.

Phantom took my hand with Rush and turned us intangible, running through the madness to our goal. We ran up the stairs of the warehouse. What is up with villains and warehouses? When I asked Phantom that he told me in a not-so nice way to shut my mouth. My breath came in short gasps as we ran up and up to the top floor.

"Are you sure he's gon' be at the top?" Rush inquired.

Phantom just told him to shut up. I pouted because he told me to shut my trap in a most ungentlemanly of ways yet to Rush it was just a 'shut up' muttered under his breath. I had to focus as a giant something that wasn't even close to human crashed into the wall and ran right through us. My heart started since I wasn't paying attention.

"KELSEY!" I heard a screech.

My ears rang and I broke free of Phantom's gloved grasp and sprinted towards the sound.

"Chaos! That's Doctor's power! Don't listen!" Rush yelled.

"Kelsey help me! It hurts!" Anna's voice screamed.

My heart was ripped apart by its seams. What would he be doing to her? My mind wandered into the darkest pit my childhood created.

"Anna!" I screamed. "I'm here!"

Something slammed into me with such force I wasn't ready for the impact. My body slammed against the brick wall. I heaved for air as I collapsed on the dirty ground.

"Hello Miss Jerrs. It is about time I meet the girl who has caught my nephew's heart. I must say, you're prettier than I expected even if blood runs down your face," a deep voice laughed. I heard the tap of expensive shoes against the concrete ground come towards me.

"Do you want to know what I have done to your friend?" he asked when he stood in front of me. His hair was salt and peppered, gelled back into a style. He wore a suit underneath a lab coat. His eyes were bright blue and I could see where Phantom got his looks.

"Your mother is on the floor above us, hanging out with whatever is left of your BFF. I hope you don't mind but I just wanted to meet you. I guess you intrigued my curiosity enough for me to become somewhat impatient. Aren't you the smart one out of the two? Surely you should have been more on guard. You know what scholars chime, expect the unexpected."

"Screw you!" I screamed, throwing my combat boot to his crotch.

He caught my foot easily within his grasp, "You're quite immature. What does my nephew see in you? I have been wondering for quite some time."

He twisted my ankle to the left so that I heard it pop. Pain shot throughout my entire leg and I screamed.

"You're weak," he stated as he backhanded me into the wall. I felt my skin tear open and the blood ooze from the back of my head.

I forced my eyes to stay on him, watching what he'd do next. As he walked towards me again, I darted to the right, stumbling to my feet and running towards the stairs. I knew that there was no way I would be able to win this fight but I needed to get Anna so badly that I ignored the pain of my ankle.

The chaos of the villains and heroes sounded closer as they got further up in the warehouse. Their progress was part of my progress. I wondered briefly where Phantom and Rush were but Doctor grabbed onto a fistful of my hair, pulling me towards him again.

"Interesting. Should I break your leg?" he asked like I was going to answer him.

Instead I just shot him my death glare. He only chuckled, "My children all give me that same look. I do not expect anything else from Maine's flesh and blood."

"She's not my mother!" I yelled as he slammed my body to the ground, hand still wrapped in my hair. I grunted and then phased through his body. I turned solid enough the shoot a small green orb from my hand to his back, pushing him onto the ground.

I climbed on top of him so I could roll him over to punch his face, "Give me Anna!"

He grunted punching me in the ribs. I didn't even feel it, being too busy whacking him as hard as I could. "Where is she?"

He flipped us so I was on the ground. Rather than punching me, he just held my face to the ground, "Did you know that the average human can lose 40% of their blood before they die? Now how would science know that? Who would they test that on?"

"You're sick!" I screamed, making him lift up my head enough to slam it back into the concrete. Blood sprayed as I totally bit my tongue hard. I coughed on the liquid.

"Let her go!" Phantom yelled, pushing a person down the stairs with a kick of his boot.

"Nice of you to join the party Colton. But it's too late for her friend."

My blood chilled as Phantom asked the question that was on the tip of my tongue, "What do you mean?"

"KELSEY!" I heard Anna scream. I swallowed the lump in my throat and phased through the floor, letting Phantom charge the Doctor and whack him with one of his green light beams.

"Go to her!" Phantom yelled at me. I phase through the two, hovering since my ankle throbbed with intense pain. I gripped the stair rail and pulled myself up the stairs, feet off the ground. I wasn't the best at hovering so the grip of the railing was very useful.

I heard Phantom struggle with Doctor. He groaned as the Doctor clipped him in the ribs with his knee. I couldn't focus on him at the moment, too busy hefting myself up the stairs.

Anna's scream pierced my ears. I yelled at her that I was coming but at that moment my entourage Phantom gathered came through the stairs. I could only hope that they would help him beat Doctor.

I finally made it and floated to where I saw a figure huddled in the far corner.

"Anna?" I asked, reaching out my hand towards the heap of blankets. There wasn't any sign that she was there but It could have been.

"She's not there," Maine stepped from out of the shadows just like a cliche movie. I could smell the scent of apple pie waft from her even though I was somewhat far away. It made my stomach churn.

"Where is she?" I growled, whipping around to face her.

Maine only cackled, but did not answer my question, "Come see your mother."

"No."

She looked hurt at my outright refusal, "But Aaron needs to see you! I want him to see you..."

"Aaron Cardinale?" I asked tentatively.

She smiled at me, "Bingo! All of the Cardinales are here in this warehouse trying to protect their daddy. I think that Colton and Mark are rebelling. They do not agree with the Brotherhood but there is nothing that they can do. Aaron will only wipe them out. Their blood will blanket the concrete floor and I cannot wait to see it. Do you think Colton's blood is green like ectoplasm?"

I moved forward to make my fist connect with the side of her face. She groaned but did not move so I punched her again. She laughed.

"Kelsey!" Rush stomped up the stairs, morphing into a bear, its jaw latching onto Maine's shoulder. She cried out in pain but then just kept laughing.

Rush knocked her over to the floor and that is how I saw my mother wince in pain and then she dissolved. Now she's dissolved before. It's her superpower. Well part of it anyways. She turns into liquid. She didn't use it often. I had only seen it twice before because turning into liquid is not something that is very useful. Her jail cell was the only place that she couldn't get out of because of the power inhibitors...

Phantom had the necklace. I gasped at the realization that if he could put it on the Doctor, then we might stand a change to get Anna.

Rush seemed to handle Maine better than I could. I floated over to the stairwell, "Phantom!" I yelled, "You have the necklace, right? Use it!"

His green eyes met mine and he reached in a pocket of his dress slacks. Maine rammed into me, making me tumble down the metal stairs. The breathe was knocked out of my lungs and suddenly my brain felt an intense pressure. I was on the concrete floor, curled into a little ball, hands pressing to the sides of my skull. It was so painful, my vision had stars.

"Stop!" Phantom cried out, slamming into the Doctor. I blinked, my vision clearing up long enough for me to see him put the power inhibitor around the Doctor's neck. Immediately my head cleared up, the pain going away. Phantom ran towards me, pulling me up from the floor and heading up the stairs.

"Anna," I groaned.

"I know, I know. We'll get her. Hurry before he takes it off."

"Should have handcuffed him to the railing," I muttered.

"I left them in your dingy van," he sighed.

I hummed, "Must not be an Eagle Scout then. You're never prepared."

He just chuckled and shook his head.

"Ugh, I do not feel so hot right now. I feel stupid, like I'm not doing anything. I am a superhero you know. I can fight villains. Why can't I help defeat Maine and Doctor? Do I need to lean on you and Rush?"

"You're okay. You're goal is not to fight but to find Anna. These people here are here to help you out so let them."

"I found Anigirl!" a villain yelled.

I turned my head around so fast it hurt. She was there, in the arms of a very big man with lots of tattoos. Blood covered her clothes an I screamed.

Phantom locked his arms around me so I couldn't escape unless I phased through him but I didn't even think about that as I struggled against him.

"Is she okay?" I asked, already knowing the answer.

She wasn't.

Chapter 29

It has been three weeks since the fight. Anna is in a coma and my life has lost all meaning. When we found her Rush in his fury killed the Doctor. That is a scene one came never forget: seeing a grown man get mutilated until he is unrecognizable. His limbs being thrown around like they're pins. I see the scene every single time I close my eyes. Makes my nights restless and my body drained of any energy.

Mrs. and Mr. Henderson are still in the dark about what happened to their little girl. I couldn't tell them my mother did that to her. I couldn't tell them anything at all. Instead I just watched them miss work and exercising to mope around the house and ask questions that I know the answer to yet couldn't explain.

I put away Chaos for good. All she causes is chaos that I cannot live with. I shredded my maxi skirts in a frenzy of anger. Other media stated that I died and in some ways I have. I think I killed Chaos the moment I saw Anna broken and limp. That part of me is smothered and I swear never to use my powers again unless it is to kill Maine.

Maine. Every time I picture that woman a white hot burning pit gathers in my stomach. On nights I plug in the Metallica album she gave me, letting the noise fill the silent downstairs. Exit light, enter night sounds about right. There is no light in the Henderson household anymore. I don't think I mind.

I think it was Mrs. Henderson who swiped the album off of my phone and off of the communal computer. I woke up one day to find my Metallica gone. It wasn't like I had the energy to care about it. I had the words engrained in my mind and did not need the CD to keep me insane.

Insane. Was I going insane? Mrs. Henderson stopped eating right, drowning her worries in the Ben & Jerry's she nicks from the mini fridge downstairs. Mr. Henderson rarely comes home but when he does he never looks at me. I don't think I'm welcomed in their home anymore but there's is nowhere else for me to go. I visit Anna everyday when I'm supposed to be in school. My grades are plummeting so hard I don't think I'll graduate. I'm okay with that.

I lie on my bed and stare up at the picture of Phantom. He's running with Rush so the Brotherhood and the Cardinales won't be able to kill him. The news found out that the head of the Cardinale family was found in pieces like a jigsaw puzzle. Nobody knows the whole story. They don't want to. Because the story seems happy at first. It seems like a lot of build up happens for this big fight that isn't such a fight at all. A person's hard work is wasted if they cannot save the one person in the world that means too much to them.

This ain't a story. It's real life. And sometimes in real life things are never fully tied up. There are too many broken strings, too many unanswered questions, too much anger.

And that, I think, is why I need to be Kelsey for a long while.

Epilogue

"You know you're unable to graduate now Miss Jerrs," the counselor tells me. I sit in a hard chair staring at my interlocked fingers in my lap. I know this already. I did the math. I didn't take the finals.

"Is something wrong?" the counselor asks me. She walks over towards where I sit and puts a hand on my hands. "You can tell me," she whispers.

I shake my head violently. I cannot tell her anything about what I have been through. It's been one month and Anna still hasn't woken up and Phantom hasn't come back. Nothing seems like it should be anymore.

"Do you have any plans?" she asks, trying to change the subject to a different topic. One that isn't to depressing.

I nod my head, "I'm leaving St. Louis."

She raises an eyebrow, "Where are you going?"

"Not sure," I state simply. I do know I want to go some-where sunny. Wherever that is is where the ten O'clock train takes me as I hitch a ride unbeknownst to the conductor.

She sighs but it's not with frustration. It's just a sigh with no deeper meaning, "That would be good for you to get away from here and start fresh. You could even attend an apprentice school."

I give her a look. Furthering my education was the last thing on my mind. She got the hint and smiled at me nonetheless.

"You have a great mind Kelsey. It would be a shame if that were to go to waste."

It wasn't on my plan to waste it. Just not with college.

I was going to find Maine and take her out. No matter the cost. I know that I cannot be Chaos anymore but that's okay. I don't have to be her to kill my mother. I can be whoever I want to be in order to get the job done. I don't need Phantom's help anymore, and it's not like he'd risk his life to come see me anyways. I'll be myself when I finally do kill Maine, forever branding myself as something I'd never thought I would be.

A villain.